Praise for *Warbreaker*

"Epic fantasy heavyweight Sanderson (The Mistborn series) pens a powerful stand-alone tale of unpredictable loyalties, dark intrigue, and dangerous magic.... Sanderson melds complex, believable characters, a marvelous world and thoughtful, ironic humor into an extraordinary and highly entertaining story."

—*Publishers Weekly* (Starred Review)

"Lets Sanderson show off what he does best.... Beyond shining as a world-building exercise, *Warbreaker*'s drama is peppered with excellent humor. With so much to love, it's easy to wish for a sequel, but hard to imagine a better ending."

—*The Onion A.V. Club* (Best of 2009)

"A highly readable and compelling stand-alone volume from the acclaimed author of the Mistborn trilogy.... Highly recommended to fans of epic fantasy."

—*Romantic Times*

"Sanderson is clearly a master of large-scale stories, splendidly depicting worlds as well as strong females, divine and mortal— to a far higher degree than one expects of much fantasy these days. May the author write long and prosper."

—*Booklist*

"Anyone looking for a different and refreshing fantasy novel will be delighted by this exceptional tale of magic, mystery and the politics of divinity. It's fair to say *Warbreaker* might even take your breath away!"

—Michael Moorcock, author of the Elric series

Tachyon Publications
1459 18th Street #139
San Francisco, CA 94107
(415) 285-5615
www.tachyonpublications.com
tachyon@tachyonpublications.com

Series Editor: Jacob Weisman
Project Editor: Jill Roberts
Copyeditor: Marty Halpern

ISBN 13: 978-1-61696-092-6
ISBN 10: 1-61696-092-2

Printed in the United States of America by Worzalla
First Edition: November 2012

9 8 7 6 5 4 3 2 1

Praise for *Elantris*

"*Elantris* is the finest novel of fantasy to be written in many years. Brandon Sanderson has created a truly original world of magic and intrigue, and with the rigor of the best science fiction writers, he has made it real at every level."

—Orson Scott Card, author of *Ender's Game*

"Sanderson's outstanding fantasy debut, refreshing complete unto itself and free of the usual genre clichés, offers something for everyone: mystery, magic, romance, political wrangling, religious conflict, fights for equality, sharp writing, and wonderful, robust characters."

—*Publishers Weekly* (Starred Review)

"The author's skill at turning conventional fantasy on its head produces a tale filled with surprising twists and turns and a conclusion both satisfying and original. Libraries of all sizes should add this to their fantasy collection."

—*Library Journal* (Starred Review)

"Brandon Sanderson's *Elantris* is a marvelous, magic monster of a book, packed full of intrigue and daring, based around a killer high concept…. All this and a genuinely touching love story too. *Elantris*, the book that put epic back into fantasy."

—Simon R. Green, author of the Deathstalker series

"*Elantris* is a well-told, character-driven story. It's also that rarest of creatures: a done-in-one-volume fantasy…although there is room for a sequel. If readers are fortunate, Sanderson will return to Arelon soon."

—*Starlog*

BRANDON SANDERSON
THE EMPEROR'S SOUL

TACHYON || SAN FRANCISCO

For Lucie Tuan and Sherry Wang,
who provided inspiration.

THE EMPEROR'S SOUL

Prologue

GAOTONA RAN HIS FINGERS across the thick canvas, inspecting one of the greatest works of art he had ever seen. Unfortunately, it was a lie.

"The woman is a danger." Hissed voices came from behind him. "What she does is an abomination."

Gaotona tipped the canvas toward the hearth's orange-red light, squinting. In his old age, his eyes weren't what they had once been. *Such precision,* he thought, inspecting the brush strokes, feeling the layers of thick oils. Exactly like those in the original.

He would never have spotted the mistakes on his own. A blossom slightly out of position. A moon that was just a sliver too low in the sky. It had taken their experts days of detailed inspection to find the errors.

"She is one of the best Forgers alive." The voices belonged to Gaotona's fellow arbiters, the empire's most important bureaucrats. "She has a reputation as wide as the empire. We need to execute her as an example."

"No." Frava, leader of the arbiters, had a sharp, nasal voice. "She is a valuable tool. This woman can save us. We must use her."

Why? Gaotona thought again. *Why would someone capable of this artistry, this majesty, turn to forgery? Why not create original paintings? Why not be a true artist?*

I must understand.

"Yes," Frava continued, "the woman is a thief, and she practices a horrid art. But I can control her, and with her talents we can fix this mess we have found ourselves in."

The others murmured worried objections. The woman they spoke of, Wan ShaiLu, was more than a simple con artist. So much more. She could change the nature of reality itself. That raised another question. Why would she bother learning to paint? Wasn't ordinary art mundane compared to her mystical talents?

So many questions. Gaotona looked up from his seat beside the hearth. The others stood in a conspiratorial clump around Frava's desk, their long, colorful robes shimmering in the firelight. "I agree with Frava," Gaotona said.

The others glanced at him. Their scowls indicated they cared little for what he said, but their postures told a different tale. Their respect for him was buried deep, but it was remembered.

"Send for the Forger," Gaotona said, rising. "I would hear what she has to say. I suspect she will be more difficult to control than Frava claims, but we have no choice. We either use this woman's skill, or we give up control of the empire."

The murmurs ceased. How many years had it been since Frava and Gaotona had agreed on anything at all, let alone on something so divisive as making use of the Forger?

One by one, the other three arbiters nodded.

"Let it be done," Frava said softly.

Day Two

SHAI PRESSED HER FINGERNAIL into one of the stone blocks of her prison cell. The rock gave way slightly. She rubbed the dust between her fingers. Limestone. An odd material for use in a prison wall, but the whole wall wasn't of limestone, merely that single vein within the block.

She smiled. Limestone. That little vein had been easy to miss, but if she was right about it, she had finally identified all forty-four types of rock in the wall of her circular pit of a prison cell. Shai knelt down beside her bunk, using a fork—she'd bent back all of the tines but one—to carve notes into the wood of one bed leg. Without her spectacles, she had to squint as she wrote.

To Forge something, you had to know its past, its nature. She was almost ready. Her pleasure quickly slipped away, however, as she noticed another set of markings on the bed leg, lit by her flickering candle. Those kept track of her days of imprisonment.

So little time, she thought. If her count was right, only a day remained before the date set for her public execution.

Deep inside, her nerves were drawn as tight as strings on an instrument. One day. One day remaining to create a soulstamp and escape. But she had no soulstone, only a crude piece of wood, and her only tool for carving was a fork.

It would be incredibly difficult. That was the point. This cell was meant for one of her kind, built of stones with many different veins of rock in them to make them difficult to Forge. They would come from different quarries and each have unique histories. Knowing as little as she did, Forging them would be nearly impossible. And even if she did transform the rock, there was probably some other failsafe to stop her.

Nights! What a mess she'd gotten herself into.

Notes finished, she found herself looking at her bent fork. She'd begun carving the wooden handle, after prying off the metal portion, as a crude soulstamp. *You're not going to get out this way, Shai,* she told herself. *You need another method.*

She'd waited six days, searching for another way out. Guards to exploit, someone to bribe, a hint about the nature of her cell. So far, nothing had—

Far above, the door to the dungeons opened.

Shai leaped to her feet, tucking the fork handle into her waistband at the small of her back. Had they moved up her execution?

Heavy boots sounded on the steps leading into the dungeon, and she squinted at the newcomers who appeared above her cell. Four were guards, accompanying a man with long features and fingers. A Grand, the race who led the empire. That robe of blue and green indicated a minor functionary who had passed the tests for government service, but not risen high in its ranks.

Shai waited, tense.

The Grand leaned down to look at her through the grate. He paused for just a moment, then waved for the guards to unlock it. "The arbiters wish to interrogate you, Forger."

Shai stood back as they opened her cell's ceiling, then lowered a ladder. She climbed, wary. If *she* were going to take someone to an early execution, she'd have let the prisoner think something else was happening, so she wouldn't resist. However, they didn't lock Shai in manacles as they marched her out of the dungeons.

Judging by their route, they did indeed seem to be taking her toward the arbiters' study. Shai composed herself. A new challenge, then. Dared she hope for an opportunity? She shouldn't have been caught, but she could do nothing about that now. She had been bested, betrayed by the Imperial Fool when she'd assumed she could trust him. He had taken her copy of the Moon Scepter and swapped it for the original, then run off.

Shai's Uncle Won had taught her that being bested was a rule of life. No matter how good you were, someone was better. Live by that knowledge, and you would never grow so confident that you became sloppy.

Last time she had lost. This time she would win. She abandoned all sense of frustration at being captured and became the person who could deal with this new chance, whatever it was. She would seize it and thrive.

This time, she played not for riches, but for her life.

The guards were Strikers—or, well, that was the Grand name for them. They had once called themselves Mulla'dil, but their nation had been folded into the empire so long ago that few used the name. Strikers were a tall people with a lean musculature and pale skin. They had hair almost as dark as Shai's, though theirs curled while hers lay straight and long. She tried with some success not to feel dwarfed by them. Her people, the MaiPon, were not known for their stature.

"You," she said to the lead Striker as she walked at the front of the group. "I remember you." Judging by that styled hair, the youthful captain did not often wear a helmet. Strikers were well regarded by the Grands, and their Elevation was not unheard of. This one had a look of eagerness to him. That polished armor, that crisp air. Yes, he fancied himself bound for important things in the future.

"The horse," Shai said. "You threw me over the back of your horse after I was captured. Tall animal, Gurish descent, pure white. Good animal. You know your horseflesh."

The Striker kept his eyes forward, but whispered under his breath, "I'm going to enjoy killing you, woman."

Lovely, Shai thought as they entered the Imperial Wing of the palace. The stonework here was marvelous, after the ancient Lamio style, with tall pillars of marble inlaid with reliefs. Those large urns between the pillars had been created to mimic Lamio pottery from long ago.

Actually, she reminded herself, *the Heritage Faction still rules, so . . .*

The emperor would be from that faction, as would the council of five arbiters who did much of the actual ruling. Their faction lauded the glory and learning of past cultures, even going so far as to rebuild their wing of the palace as an imitation of an ancient building. Shai suspected that on the bottoms of those "ancient" urns would be soulstamps that had transformed them into perfect imitations of famous pieces.

Yes, the Grands called Shai's powers an abomination, but the only aspect of it that was technically illegal was creating a Forgery to change a person. Quiet Forgery of objects was allowed, even exploited, in the empire so long as the Forger was carefully controlled. If someone were to turn over one of those urns and remove the stamp on the bottom, the piece would become simple unornamented pottery.

The Strikers led her to a door with gold inlay. As it opened, she managed to catch a glimpse of the red soulstamp on the bottom inside edge, transforming the door into an imitation of some work from the past. The guards ushered her into a homey room with a crackling hearth, deep rugs, and stained wood furnishings. *Fifth century hunting lodge,* she guessed.

All five arbiters of the Heritage Faction waited inside. Three—two women, one man—sat in tall-backed chairs at the hearth. One other woman occupied the desk just inside the doors: Frava, senior among the arbiters of the Heritage Faction, was probably the most powerful person in the empire other than Emperor Ashravan himself. Her greying hair was woven into a long braid with gold and red ribbons; it draped a robe of matching gold. Shai had long pondered how to rob this woman, as—among her duties—Frava oversaw the Imperial Gallery and had offices adjacent to it.

Frava had obviously been arguing with Gaotona, the elderly male Grand standing beside the desk. He stood up straight and clasped his hands behind his back in a thoughtful pose. Gaotona was eldest of the ruling arbiters. He was said to be the least influential among them, out of favor with the emperor.

Both fell silent as Shai entered. They eyed her as if

she were a cat that had just knocked over a fine vase. Shai missed her spectacles, but took care not to squint as she stepped up to face these people; she needed to look as strong as possible.

"Wan ShaiLu," Frava said, reaching to pick up a sheet of paper from the desk. "You have quite the list of crimes credited to your name."

The way you say that . . . What game was this woman playing? *She wants something of me,* Shai decided. *That is the only reason to bring me in like this.*

The opportunity began to unfold.

"Impersonating a noblewoman of rank," Frava continued, "breaking into the palace's Imperial Gallery, reForging your soul, and of course the attempted theft of the Moon Scepter. Did you really assume that we would fail to recognize a simple forgery of such an important imperial possession?"

Apparently, Shai thought, *you have done just that, assuming that the Fool escaped with the original.* It gave Shai a little thrill of satisfaction to know that her forgery now occupied the Moon Scepter's position of honor in the Imperial Gallery.

"And what of this?" Frava said, waving long fingers for one of the Strikers to bring something from the side of the room. A painting, which the guard placed on the desk. Han ShuXen's masterpiece *Lily of the Spring Pond.*

"We found this in your room at the inn," Frava said,

tapping her fingers on the painting. "It is a copy of a painting I myself own, one of the most famous in the empire. We gave it to our assessors, and they judge that your forgery was amateur at best."

Shai met the woman's eyes.

"Tell me why you have created this forgery," Frava said, leaning forward. "You were obviously planning to swap this for the painting in my office by the Imperial Gallery. And yet, you were striving for the *Moon Scepter* itself. Why plan to steal the painting too? Greed?"

"My uncle Won," Shai said, "told me to always have a backup plan. I couldn't be certain the scepter would even be on display."

"Ah . . ." Frava said. She adopted an almost maternal expression, though it was laden with loathing—hidden poorly—and condescension. "You requested arbiter intervention in your execution, as most prisoners do. I decided on a whim to agree to your request because I was curious why you had created this painting." She shook her head. "But child, you can't honestly believe we'd let you free. With sins like this? You are in a monumentally bad predicament, and our mercy can only be extended so far . . ."

Shai glanced toward the other arbiters. The ones seated near the fireplace seemed to be paying no heed, but they did not speak to one another. They were listening. *Something is wrong*, Shai thought. *They're worried.*

Gaotona still stood just to the side. He inspected Shai with eyes that betrayed no emotion.

Frava's manner had the air of one scolding a small child. The lingering end of her comment was intended to make Shai hope for release. Together, that was meant to make her pliable, willing to agree to anything in the hope that she'd be freed.

An opportunity indeed . . .

It was time to take control of this conversation.

"You want something from me," Shai said. "I'm ready to discuss my payment."

"Your *payment?*" Frava asked. "Girl, you are to be executed on the morrow! If we did wish something of you, the payment would be your life."

"My life is my own," Shai said. "And it has been for days now."

"Please," Frava said. "You were locked in the Forger's cell, with thirty different kinds of stone in the wall."

"Forty-four kinds, actually."

Gaotona raised an appreciative eyebrow.

Nights! I'm glad I got that right . . .

Shai glanced at Gaotona. "You thought I wouldn't recognize the grindstone, didn't you? Please. I'm a Forger. I learned stone classification during my first year of training. That block was obviously from the Laio quarry."

Frava opened her mouth to speak, a slight smile to her lips.

"Yes, I know about the plates of ralkalest, the unForgeable metal, hidden behind the rock wall of my cell," Shai guessed. "The wall was a puzzle, meant to distract me. You wouldn't *actually* make a cell out of rocks like limestone, just in case a prisoner gave up on Forgery and tried to chip their way free. You built the wall, but secured it with a plate of ralkalest at the back to cut off escape."

Frava snapped her mouth shut.

"The problem with ralkalest," Shai said, "is that it's not a very strong metal. Oh, the grate at the top of my cell was solid enough, and I couldn't have gotten through that. But a thin plate? Really. Have you heard of anthracite?"

Frava frowned.

"It is a rock that burns," Gaotona said.

"You gave me a candle," Shai said, reaching into the small of her back. She tossed her makeshift wooden soulstamp onto the desk. "All I had to do was Forge the wall and persuade the stones that they're anthracite— not a difficult task, once I knew the forty-four types of rock. I could burn them, and they'd melt that plate behind the wall."

Shai pulled over a chair, seating herself before the desk. She leaned back. Behind her, the captain of the Strikers growled softly, but Frava drew her lips to a line and said nothing. Shai let her muscles relax, and she breathed a quiet prayer to the Unknown God.

Nights! It looked like they'd actually bought it. She'd worried they'd know enough of Forgery to see through her lie.

"I was going to escape tonight," Shai said, "but whatever it is you want me to do must be important, as you're willing to involve a miscreant like myself. And so we come to my payment."

"I could still have you executed," Frava said. "Right now. Here."

"But you won't, will you?"

Frava set her jaw.

"I warned you that she would be difficult to manipulate," Gaotona said to Frava. Shai could tell she'd impressed him, but at the same time, his eyes seemed . . . sorrowful? Was that the right emotion? She found this aged man as difficult to read as a book in Svordish.

Frava raised a finger, then swiped it to the side. A servant approached with a small, cloth-wrapped box. Shai's heart leaped upon seeing it.

The man clicked the latches open on the front and raised the top. The case was lined with soft cloth and inset with five depressions made to hold soulstamps. Each cylindrical stone stamp was as long as a finger and as wide as a large man's thumb. The leatherbound notebook set in the case atop them was worn by long use; Shai breathed in a hint of its familiar scent.

They were called Essence Marks, the most powerful

kind of soulstamp. Each Essence Mark had to be attuned to a specific individual, and was intended to rewrite their history, personality, and soul for a short time. These five were attuned to Shai.

"Five stamps to rewrite a soul," Frava said. "Each is an abomination, illegal to possess. These Essence Marks were to be destroyed this afternoon. Even if you had escaped, you'd have lost these. How long does it take to create one?"

"Years," Shai whispered.

There were no other copies. Notes and diagrams were too dangerous to leave, even in secret, as such things gave others too much insight to one's soul. She never let these Essence Marks out of her sight, except on the rare occasion they were taken from her.

"You will accept these as payment?" Frava asked, lips turned down, as if discussing a meal of slime and rotted meat.

"Yes."

Frava nodded, and the servant snapped the case closed. "Then let me show you what you are to do."

Shai had never met an emperor before, let alone poked one in the face.

Emperor Ashravan of the Eighty Suns—forty-ninth

ruler of the Rose Empire—did not respond as Shai prodded him. He stared ahead blankly, his round cheeks rosy and hale, but his expression completely lifeless.

"What happened?" Shai asked, straightening from beside the emperor's bed. It was in the style of the ancient Lamio people, with a headboard shaped like a phoenix rising toward heaven. She'd seen a sketch of such a headboard in a book; likely the Forgery had been drawn from that source.

"Assassins," Arbiter Gaotona said. He stood on the other side of the bed, alongside two surgeons. Of the Strikers, only their captain—Zu—had been allowed to enter. "The murderers broke in two nights ago, attacking the emperor and his wife. She was slain. The emperor received a crossbow bolt to the head."

"That considered," Shai noted, "he's looking remarkable."

"You are familiar with resealing?" Gaotona asked.

"Vaguely," Shai said. Her people called it Flesh Forgery. Using it, a surgeon of great skill could Forge a body to remove its wounds and scars. It required great specialization. The Forger had to know each and every sinew, each vein and muscle, in order to accurately heal.

Resealing was one of the few branches of Forgery that Shai hadn't studied in depth. Get an ordinary forgery wrong, and you created a work of poor artistic merit. Get a Flesh Forgery wrong, and people died.

"Our resealers are the best in the world," Frava said,

walking around the foot of the bed, hands behind her back. "The emperor was attended to quickly following the assassination attempt. The wound to his head was healed, but . . ."

"But his mind was not?" Shai asked, waving her hand in front of the man's face again. "It doesn't sound like they did a very good job at all."

One of the surgeons cleared his throat. The diminutive man had ears like window shutters that had been thrown open wide on a sunny day. "Resealing repairs a body and makes it anew. That, however, is much like rebinding a book with fresh paper following a fire. Yes, it may look exactly the same, and it may be whole all the way through. The words, though . . . the words are gone. We have given the emperor a new brain. It is merely empty."

"Huh," Shai said. "Did you find out who tried to kill him?"

The five arbiters exchanged glances. Yes, they knew.

"We are not certain," Gaotona said.

"Meaning," Shai added, "you know, but you couldn't prove it well enough to make an accusation. One of the other factions in court, then?"

Gaotona sighed. "The Glory Faction."

Shai whistled softly, but it *did* make sense. If the emperor died, there was a good chance that the Glory Faction would win a bid to elevate his successor. At forty, Emperor Ashravan was young still, by Grand standards. He had been expected to rule another fifty years.

If he were replaced, the five arbiters in this room would lose their positions—which, by imperial politics, would be a huge blow to their status. They'd drop from being the most powerful people in the world to being among the lowest of the empire's eighty factions.

"The assassins did not survive their attack," Frava said. "The Glory Faction does not yet know whether their ploy succeeded. You are going to replace the emperor's soul with . . ." She took a deep breath. "With a Forgery."

They're crazy, Shai thought. Forging one's own soul was difficult enough, and you didn't have to rebuild it from the ground up.

The arbiters had no idea what they were asking. But of course they didn't. They hated Forgery, or so they claimed. They walked on imitation floor tiles past copies of ancient vases, they let their surgeons repair a body, but they didn't call any of these things "Forgery" in their own tongue.

The Forgery of the soul, that was what they considered an abomination. Which meant Shai really was their only choice. No one in their own government would be capable of this. She probably wasn't either.

"Can you do it?" Gaotona asked.

I have no idea, Shai thought. "Yes," she said.

"It will need to be an exact Forgery," Frava said

sternly. "If the Glory Faction has any inkling of what we've done, they will pounce. The emperor must not act erratically."

"I said I could do it," Shai replied. "But it will be difficult. I will need information about Ashravan and his life, everything we can get. Official histories will be a start, but they'll be too sterile. I will need extensive interviews and writings about him from those who knew him best. Servants, friends, family members. Did he have a journal?"

"Yes," Gaotona said.

"Excellent."

"Those documents are sealed," said one of the other arbiters. "He wanted them destroyed . . ."

Everyone in the room looked toward the man. He swallowed, then looked down.

"You shall have everything you request," Frava said.

"I'll need a test subject as well," Shai said. "Someone to test my Forgeries on. A Grand, male, someone who was around the emperor a lot and who knew him. That will let me see if I have the personality right." Nights! Getting the personality right would be secondary. Getting a stamp that actually took . . . that would be the first step. She wasn't certain she could manage even that much. "And I'll need soulstone, of course."

Frava regarded Shai, arms folded.

"You can't possibly expect me to do this without soulstone," Shai said drily. "I could carve a stamp out of wood, if I had to, but your goal will be difficult enough as it is. Soulstone. Lots of it."

"Fine," Frava said. "But you will be watched these three months. Closely."

"Three *months?*" Shai said. "I'm planning for this to take at least two years."

"You have a hundred days," Frava said. "Actually, ninety-eight, now."

Impossible.

"The official explanation for why the emperor hasn't been seen these last two days," said one of the other arbiters, "is that he's been in mourning for the death of his wife. The Glory Faction will assume we are scrambling to buy time following the emperor's death. Once the hundred days of isolation are finished, they will demand that Ashravan present himself to the court. If he does not, we are finished."

And so are you, the woman's tone implied.

"I will need gold for this," Shai said. "Take what you're thinking I'll demand and double it. I will walk out of this country rich."

"Done," Frava said.

Too easy, Shai thought. Delightful. They were planning to kill her once this was done.

Well, that gave her ninety-eight days to find a way out. "Get me those records," she said. "I'll need a place to work, plenty of supplies, and my things back." She held up a finger before they could complain. "Not my

Essence Marks, but everything else. I'm not going to work for three months in the same clothing I've been wearing while in prison. And, as I consider it, have someone draw me a bath immediately."

Day Three

THE NEXT DAY—bathed, well fed, and well rested for the first time since her capture—Shai received a knock at her door.

They'd given her a room. It was tiny, probably the most drab in the entire palace, and it smelled faintly of mildew. They had still posted guards to watch her all night, of course, and—from her memory of the layout of the vast palace—she was in one of the least frequented wings, one used mostly for storage.

Still, it was better than a cell. Barely.

At the knock, Shai looked up from her inspection of the room's old cedar table. It probably hadn't seen an oiling cloth in longer than Shai had been alive. One of her guards opened the door, letting in the elderly Arbiter Gaotona. He carried a box two handspans wide and a couple of inches deep.

Shai rushed over, drawing a glare from Captain Zu,

who stood beside the arbiter. "Keep your distance from his grace," Zu growled.

"Or what?" Shai asked, taking the box. "You'll stab me?"

"Someday, I will enjoy—"

"Yes, yes," Shai said, walking back to her table and flipping open the box's lid. Inside were eighteen soul-stamps, their heads smooth and unetched. She felt a thrill and picked one up, holding it out and inspecting it.

She had her spectacles back now, so no more squinting. She also wore clothing far more fitting than that dingy dress. A flat, red, calf-length skirt and buttoned blouse. The Grands would consider it unfashionable, as among them, ancient-looking robes or wraps were the current style. Shai found those dreary. Under the blouse she wore a tight cotton shirt, and under the skirt she wore leggings. A lady never knew when she might need to ditch her outer layer of clothing to effect a disguise.

"This is good stone," Shai said of the stamp in her fingers. She took out one of her chisels, which had a tip almost as fine as a pinhead, and began to scrape at the rock. It *was* good soulstone. The rock came away easily and precisely. Soulstone was almost as soft as chalk, but did not chip when scraped. You could carve it with high precision, and then set it with a flame and a mark on the top, which would harden it to a strength closer to quartz. The only way to get a better stamp was to carve one from crystal itself, which was incredibly difficult.

For ink, they had provided bright red squid's ink, mixed with a small percentage of wax. Any fresh organic ink would work, though inks from animals were better than inks from plants.

"Did you . . . steal a vase from the hallway outside?" Gaotona asked, frowning toward an object sitting at the side of her small room. She'd snatched one of the vases on the way back from the bath. One of her guards had tried to interfere, but Shai had talked her way past the objection. That guard was now blushing.

"I was curious about the skills of your Forgers," Shai said, setting down her tools and hauling the vase up onto the table. She turned it on its side, showing the bottom and the red seal imprinted into the clay there.

A Forger's seal was easy to spot. It didn't just imprint onto the object's surface, it actually sank *into* the material, creating a depressed pattern of red troughs. The rim of the round seal was red as well, but raised, like an embossing.

You could tell a lot about a person from the way they designed their seals. This one, for example, had a sterile feel to it. No real art, which was a contrast to the minutely detailed and delicate beauty of the vase itself. Shai had heard that the Heritage Faction kept lines of half-trained Forgers working by rote, creating these pieces like rows of men making shoes in a factory.

"Our workers are *not* Forgers," Gaotona said. "We don't use that word. They are Rememberers."

"It's the same thing."

"They don't touch souls," Gaotona said sternly. "Beyond that, what we do is in appreciation of the past, rather than with the aim of fooling or scamming people. Our reminders bring people to a greater understanding of their heritage."

Shai raised an eyebrow. She took her mallet and chisel, then brought them down at an angle on the embossed rim of the vase's seal. The seal resisted—there was a *force* to it, trying to stay in place—but the blow broke through. The rest of the seal popped up, troughs vanishing, the seal becoming simple ink and losing its powers.

The colors of the vase faded immediately, bleeding to plain grey, and its shape warped. A soulstamp didn't just make visual changes, but rewrote an object's history. Without the stamp, the vase was a horrid piece. Whoever had thrown it hadn't cared about the end product. Perhaps they'd known it would be part of a Forgery. Shai shook her head and turned back to her work on the unfinished soulstamp. This wasn't for the emperor—she wasn't nearly ready for that yet—but carving helped her think.

Gaotona gestured for the guards to leave, all but Zu, who remained by his side. "You present a puzzle, Forger," Gaotona said once the other two guards were gone, the door closed. He settled down in one of the two rickety wooden chairs. They—along with the splintery bed, the ancient table, and the trunk with her things—made up the room's entire array of furniture. The single window had a warped frame that let in the breeze, and even the walls had cracks in them.

"A puzzle?" Shai asked, holding up the stamp before her, peering closely at her work. "What kind of puzzle?"

"You are a Forger. Therefore, you cannot be trusted without supervision. You will try to run the moment you think of a practicable escape."

"So leave guards with me," Shai said, carving some more.

"Pardon," Gaotona said, "but I doubt it would take you long to bully, bribe, or blackmail them."

Nearby, Zu stiffened.

"I meant no offense, Captain," Gaotona said. "I have great confidence in your people, but what we have before us is a master trickster, liar, and thief. Your best guards would eventually become clay in her hands."

"Thank you," Shai said.

"It was *not* a compliment. What your type touches, it corrupts. I worried about leaving you alone even for one day under the supervision of mortal eyes. From what I know of you, you could nearly charm the gods themselves."

She continued working.

"I cannot trust in manacles to hold you," Gaotona

said softly, "as we are required to give you soulstone so that you can work on our . . . problem. You would turn your manacles to soap, then escape in the night laughing."

That statement, of course, betrayed a complete lack of understanding in how Forgery worked. A Forgery had to be likely—believable—otherwise it wouldn't take. Who would make a chain out of soap? It would be ridiculous.

What she *could* do, however, was discover the chain's origins and composition, then rewrite one or the other. She could Forge the chain's past so that one of the links had been cast incorrectly, which would give her a flaw to exploit. Even if she could not find the chain's exact history, she might be able to escape—an imperfect stamp would not take for long, but she'd only need a few moments to shatter the link with a mallet.

They could make a chain out of ralkalest, the un-Forgeable metal, but that would only delay her escape. With enough time, and soulstone, she would find a solution. Forging the wall to have a weak crack in it, so she could pull the chain free. Forging the ceiling to have a loose block, which she could let drop and shatter the weak ralkalest links.

She didn't want to do something so extreme if she didn't have to. "I don't see that you need to worry about me," Shai said, still working. "I am intrigued by what we are doing, and I've been promised wealth. That is enough to keep me here. Don't forget, I could have escaped my previous cell at any time."

"Ah yes," Gaotona said. "The cell in which you would have used Forgery to get through the wall. Tell me, out of curiosity, have you studied anthracite? That rock you said you'd turn the wall into? I seem to recall that it is very difficult to make burn."

This one is more clever than people give him credit for being.

A candle's flame would have trouble igniting anthracite—on paper, the rock burned at the correct temperature, but getting an entire sample hot enough was very difficult. "I was fully capable of creating a proper kindling environment with some wood from my bunk and a few rocks turned into coal."

"Without a kiln?" Gaotona said, sounding faintly amused. "With no bellows? But that is beside the point. Tell me, how were you planning to *survive* inside a cell where the wall was aflame at over two thousand degrees? Would not that kind of fire suck away all of the breathable air? Ah, but of course. You could have used your bed linens and transformed them into a poor conductor, perhaps glass, and made a shell for yourself to hide in."

Shai continued her carving, uncomfortable. The way he said that . . . Yes, he knew that she could not have done what he described. Most Grands were ignorant about the ways of Forgery, and this man certainly still was, but he *did* know enough to realize she couldn't have escaped as she said. No more than bed linens could become glass.

Beyond that, making the entire wall into another type of rock would have been difficult. She would have had to change too many things—rewritten history so that the quarries for each type of stone were near deposits of anthracite, and that in each case, a block of the burnable rock was quarried by mistake. That was a huge stretch, an almost impossible one, particularly without specific knowledge of the quarries in question.

Plausibility was key to any forgery, magical or not. People whispered of Forgers turning lead into gold, never realizing that the reverse was far, far easier. Inventing a history for a bar of gold where somewhere along the line, someone had adulterated it with lead . . . well, that was a plausible lie. The reverse would be so unlikely that a stamp to make that transformation would not take for long.

"You impress me, your grace," Shai finally said. "You think like a Forger."

Gaotona's expression soured.

"That," she noted, "*was* meant as a compliment."

"I value truth, young woman. Not Forgery." He regarded her with the expression of a disappointed grandfather. "I have seen the work of your hands. That copied painting you did . . . it was *remarkable*. Yet it was accomplished in the name of lies. What great works could you create if you focused on industry and beauty instead of wealth and deception?"

"What I do *is* great art."

"No. You copy other people's great art. What you do is technically marvelous, yet completely lacking in spirit."

She almost slipped in her carving, hands growing tense. How *dare* he? Threatening to execute her was one thing, but insulting her art? He made her sound like . . . like one of those assembly line Forgers, churning out vase after vase!

She calmed herself with difficulty, then plastered on a smile. Her aunt Sol had once told Shai to smile at the worst insults and snap at the minor ones. That way, no man would know your heart.

"So how *am* I to be kept in line?" she asked. "We have established that I am among the most vile wretches to slither through the halls of this palace. You cannot bind me and you cannot trust your own soldiers to guard me."

"Well," Gaotona said, "whenever possible, I personally will observe your work."

She would have preferred Frava—that one seemed as if she'd be easier to manipulate—but this was workable. "If you wish," Shai said. "Much of it will be boring to one who does not understand Forgery."

"I am not interested in being entertained," Gaotona said, waving one hand to Captain Zu. "Whenever I am here, Captain Zu will guard me. He is the only one of our Strikers to know the extent of the emperor's injury, and only he knows of our plan with you. Other guards will watch you during the rest of the day, and you are *not* to speak to them of your task. There will be no rumors of what we do."

"You don't need to worry about me talking," Shai said, truthfully for once. "The more people who know of a Forgery, the more likely it is to fail." *Besides*, she thought, *if I told the guards, you'd undoubtedly execute them to preserve your secrets.* She didn't like Strikers, but she liked the empire less, and the guards were really just another kind of slave. Shai wasn't in the business of getting people killed for no reason.

"Excellent," Gaotona said. "The second method of insuring your . . . attention to your project waits outside. If you would, good Captain?"

Zu opened the door. A cloaked figure stood with the guards. The figure stepped into the room; his walk was lithe, but somehow unnatural. After Zu closed the door, the figure removed his hood, revealing a face with milky white skin and red eyes.

Shai hissed softly through her teeth. "And you call what *I* do an abomination?"

Gaotona ignored her, standing up from his chair to regard the newcomer. "Tell her."

The newcomer rested long white fingers on her door, inspecting it. "I will place the rune here," he said in an accented voice. "If she leaves this room for any reason, or if she alters the rune or the door, I will know. My pets will come for her."

Shai shivered. She glared at Gaotona. "A Bloodsealer. You invited a *Bloodsealer* into your palace?"

"This one has proven himself an asset recently," Gaotona said. "He is loyal and he is discreet. He is also very effective. There are . . . times when one must accept the aid of darkness in order to contain a greater darkness."

Shai hissed softly as the Bloodsealer removed something from within his robes. A crude soulstamp created from a bone. His "pets" would also be bone, Forgeries of human life crafted from the skeletons of the dead.

The Bloodsealer looked to her.

Shai backed away. "Surely you don't expect—"

Zu took her by the arms. Nights, but he was strong. She panicked. Her Essence Marks! She needed her Essence Marks! With those, she could fight, escape, run . . .

Zu cut her along the back of her arm. She barely felt the shallow wound, but she struggled anyway. The Bloodsealer stepped up and inked his horrid tool in Shai's blood. He then turned and pressed the stamp against the center of her door.

When he withdrew his hand, he left a glowing red seal in the wood. It was shaped like an eye. The moment he marked the seal, Shai felt a sharp pain in her arm, where she'd been cut.

Shai gasped, eyes wide. Never had any person *dared* do such a thing to her. Almost better that she had been executed! Almost better that—

Control yourself, she told herself forcibly. *Become someone who can deal with this.*

She took a deep breath and let herself become someone else. An imitation of herself who was calm, even in a situation like this. It was a crude forgery, just a trick of the mind, but it worked.

She shook herself free from Zu, then accepted the kerchief Gaotona handed her. She glared at the Bloodsealer as the pain in her arm faded. He smiled at her with lips that were white and faintly translucent, like the skin of a maggot. He nodded to Gaotona before replacing his hood and stepping out of the room, closing the door after.

Shai forced herself to breathe evenly, calming herself. There was no subtlety to what the Bloodsealer did; they didn't traffic in subtlety. Instead of skill or artistry, they used tricks and blood. However, their craft was effective. The man would know if Shai left the room, and he had her fresh blood on his stamp, which was attuned to her. With that, his undead pets would be able to hunt her no matter where she ran.

Gaotona settled back down in his chair. "You know what will happen if you flee?"

Shai glared at Gaotona.

"You now realize how desperate we are," he said softly, lacing his fingers before him. "If you do run, we will give you to the Bloodsealer. Your bones will become his next pet. This promise was all he requested in payment. You may begin your work, Forger. Do it well, and you will escape this fate."

Day Five

WORK SHE DID.

Shai began digging through accounts of the emperor's life. Few people understood how much Forgery was about study and research. It was an art any man or woman could learn; it required only a steady hand and an eye for detail.

That and a willingness to spend weeks, months, even *years* preparing the ideal soulstamp.

Shai didn't have years. She felt rushed as she read biography after biography, often staying up well into the night taking notes. She did not believe that she could do what they asked of her. Creating a believable Forgery of another man's soul, particularly in such a short time, just wasn't possible. Unfortunately, she had to make a good show of it while she planned her escape.

They didn't let her leave the room. She used a chamber pot when nature called, and for baths she was allowed a tub of warm water and cloths. She was under supervision at all times, even when bathing.

That Bloodsealer came each morning to renew his mark on the door. Each time, the act required a little blood from Shai. Her arms were soon laced with shallow cuts.

All the while, Gaotona visited. The ancient arbiter studied her as she read, watching with those eyes that judged . . . but also did not hate.

As she formulated her plans, she decided one thing: getting free would probably require manipulating this man in some way.

Day Twelve

SHAI PRESSED HER STAMP down on the tabletop.

As always, the stamp sank slightly into the material. A soulstamp left a seal you could feel, regardless of the material. She twisted the stamp a half turn—this did not blur the ink, though she did not know why. One of her mentors had taught that it was because by this point the seal was touching the object's soul and not its physical presence.

When she pulled the stamp back, it left a bright red seal in the wood as if carved there. Transformation spread from the seal in a wave. The table's dull grey splintery cedar became beautiful and well maintained, with a warm patina that reflected the light of the candles sitting across from her.

Shai rested her fingers on the new table; it was now smooth to the touch. The sides and legs were finely carved, inlaid here and there with silver.

Gaotona sat upright, lowering the book he'd been reading. Zu shuffled in discomfort at seeing the Forgery.

"What was that?" Gaotona demanded.

"I was tired of getting splinters," Shai said, settling back in her chair. It creaked. *You are next,* she thought.

Gaotona stood up and walked to the table. He touched it, as if expecting the transformation to be mere illusion. It was not. The fine table now looked horribly out of place in the dingy room. "This is what you've been doing?"

"Carving helps me think."

"You should be focused on your task!" Gaotona said. "This is frivolity. The empire itself is in danger!"

No, Shai thought. *Not the empire itself; just your rule of it.* Unfortunately, after eleven days, she still didn't have an angle on Gaotona, not one she could exploit.

"I *am* working on your problem, Gaotona," she said. "What you ask of me is hardly a simple task."

"And changing that table was?"

"Of course it was," Shai said. "All I had to do was rewrite its past so that it was maintained, rather than being allowed to sink into disrepair. That took hardly any work at all."

Gaotona hesitated, then knelt beside the table. "These carvings, this inlay . . . those were not part of the original."

"I might have added a little."

She wasn't certain if the Forgery would take or not. In a few minutes, that seal might evaporate and the table might revert to its previous state. Still, she was fairly certain she'd guessed the table's past well enough. Some of the histories she was reading mentioned what gifts had come from where. This table, she suspected, had come from far-off Svorden as a gift to Emperor Ashravan's predecessor. The strained relationship with Svorden had then led the emperor to lock it away and ignore it.

"I don't recognize this piece," Gaotona said, still looking at the table.

"Why should you?"

"I have studied ancient arts extensively," he said. "This is from the Vivare dynasty?"

"No."

"An imitation of the work of Chamrav?"

"No."

"What then?"

"Nothing," Shai said with exasperation. "It's not imitating anything; it has become a better version of itself." That was a maxim of good Forgery: improve slightly on an original, and people would often accept the fake because it *was* superior.

Gaotona stood up, looking troubled. *He's thinking again that my talent is wasted,* Shai thought with annoyance, moving aside a stack of accounts of the emperor's life. Collected at her request, these came from palace servants. She didn't want only the official histories. She needed authenticity, not sterilized recitations.

Gaotona stepped back to his chair. "I do not see how transforming this table could have taken hardly any work, although it clearly must be much simpler than what you have been asked to do. Both seem incredible to me."

"Changing a human soul is far more difficult."

"I can accept that conceptually, but I do not know the specifics. Why is it so?"

She glanced at him. *He wants to know more of what I'm doing,* she thought, *so that he can tell how I'm preparing to escape.* He knew she would be trying, of course. They both would pretend that neither knew that fact.

"All right," she said, standing and walking to the wall of her room. "Let's talk about Forgery. Your cage for me had a wall of forty-four types of stone, mostly as a trap to keep me distracted. I had to figure out the makeup and origin of each block if I wanted to try to escape. Why?"

"So you could create a Forgery of the wall, obviously."

"But why all of them?" she asked. "Why not just change one block or a few? Why not just make a hole big enough to slip into, creating a tunnel for myself?"

"I . . ." He frowned. "I have no idea."

Shai rested her hand against the outer wall of her room. It had been painted, though the paint was coming off in several sections. She could feel the separate stones. "All things exist in three Realms, Gaotona. Physical, Cognitive, Spiritual. The Physical is what we feel, what is before us. The Cognitive is how an object is viewed and how it views itself. The Spiritual Realm contains an object's soul—its essence—as well as the ways it is connected to the things and people around it."

"You must understand," Gaotona said, "I don't subscribe to your pagan superstitions."

"Yes, you worship the sun instead," Shai said, failing to keep the amusement out of her voice. "Or, rather, eighty suns—believing that even though each looks the same, a different sun actually rises each day. Well, you wanted to know how Forgery works, and why the emperor's soul will be so difficult to reproduce. The Realms are important to this."

"Very well."

"Here is the point. The longer an object exists as a whole, and the longer it is *seen* in that state, the stronger its sense of complete identity becomes. That table is made up of various pieces of wood fitted together, but do we think of it that way? No. We see the whole.

"To Forge the table, I must understand it as a whole. The same goes for a wall. That wall has existed long enough to view itself as a single entity. I could, perhaps, have attacked each block separately—they might still be distinct enough—but doing so would be difficult, as the wall wants to act as a whole."

"The wall," Gaotona said flatly, "*wants* to be treated as a whole."

"Yes."

"You imply that the wall has a soul."

"All things do," she said. "Each object sees itself as something. Connection and intent are vital. This is why, master Arbiter, I can't simply write down a personality for your emperor, stamp him, and be done. Seven reports I've read say his favorite color was green. Do you know why?"

"No," Gaotona said. "Do you?"

"I'm not sure yet," Shai said. "I *think* it was because his brother, who died when Ashravan was six, had always been fond of it. The emperor latched on to it, as it reminds him of his dead sibling. There might be a touch of nationalism to it as well, as he was born in Ukurgi, where the provincial flag is predominantly green."

Gaotona seemed troubled. "You must know something that specific?"

"Nights, yes! And a thousand things just as detailed. I can get some wrong. I *will* get some wrong. Most of them, hopefully, won't matter—they will make his personality a little off, but each person changes day to day in any case. If I get too many wrong, though, the personality won't matter because the stamp won't take. At least, it won't last long enough to do any good. I assume that if your emperor has to be restamped every fifteen minutes, the charade will be impossible to maintain."

"You assume correctly."

Shai sat down with a sigh, looking over her notes.

"You said you could do this," Gaotona said.

"Yes."

"You've done it before, with your own soul."

"I know my own soul," she said. "I know my own history. I know what I can change to get the effect I need—and even getting my own Essence Marks right was difficult. Now I not only have to do this for another person, but the transformation must be far more extensive. And I have ninety days left to do it."

Gaotona nodded slowly.

"Now," she said, "you should tell me what you're doing to keep up the pretense that the emperor is still awake and well."

"We're doing all that needs to be done."

"I'm far from confident that you are. I think you'll find me a fair bit better at deception than most."

"I think that *you* will be surprised," Gaotona said. "We are, after all, politicians."

"All right, fine. But you are sending food, aren't you?"

"Of course," Gaotona said. "Three meals are sent to the emperor's quarters each day. They return to the palace kitchens eaten, though he is, of course, secretly being fed broth. He drinks it when prompted, but stares ahead, as if both deaf and mute."

"And the chamber pot?"

"He has no control over himself," Gaotona said, grimacing. "We keep him in cloth diapers."

"Nights, man! And no one changes a fake chamber pot? Don't you think that's suspicious? Maids will gossip, as will guards at the door. You need to consider these things!"

Gaotona had the decency to blush. "I will see that it happens, though I don't like the idea of someone else entering his quarters. Too many have a chance to discover what has happened to him."

"Pick someone you trust, then," Shai said. "In fact, make a rule at the emperor's doors. No one enters unless they bear a card with your personal signet. And yes, I know why you are opening your mouth to object. I know exactly how well guarded the emperor's quarters are—that was part of what I studied to break into the gallery. Your security isn't tight enough, as the assassins proved. Do what I suggest. The more layers of security, the better. If what has happened to the emperor gets out, I have no doubt that I'll end up back in that cell waiting for execution."

Gaotona sighed, but nodded. "What else do you suggest?"

Day Seventeen

A COOL BREEZE laden with unfamiliar spices crept through the cracks around Shai's warped window. The low hum of cheers seeped through as well. Outside, the city celebrated. Delbahad, a holiday no one had known about until two years earlier. The Heritage Faction continued to dig up and revive ancient feasts in an effort to sway public opinion back toward them.

It wouldn't help. The empire was not a republic, and the only ones who would have a say in anointing a new emperor would be the arbiters of the various factions. Shai turned her attention away from the celebrations, and continued to read from the emperor's journal.

I have decided, at long last, to agree to the demands of my faction, the book read. *I will offer myself for the position of emperor, as Gaotona has so often encouraged. Emperor Yazad grows weak with his disease, and a new choice will be made soon.*

Shai made a notation. Gaotona had encouraged Ashravan to seek the throne. And yet, later in the journal, Ashravan spoke of Gaotona with contempt. Why the change? She finished the notation, then turned to another entry years later.

Emperor Ashravan's personal journal fascinated her. He had written it with his own hand, and had included instructions for it to be destroyed upon his death. The arbiters had delivered the journal to her reluctantly, and with vociferous justification. He hadn't died. His body still lived. Therefore, it was just fine for them *not* to burn his writings.

They spoke with confidence, but she could see the uncertainty in their eyes. They were easy to read—all but Gaotona, whose inner thoughts continued to elude her. They didn't understand the purpose of this journal. Why write, they wondered, if not for posterity? Why put your thoughts to paper if not for the purpose of having others read them?

As easy, she thought, *to ask a Forger why she would get satisfaction from creating a fake and seeing it on display without a single person knowing it was her work—and not that of the original artist—they were revering.*

The journal told her far more about the emperor than the official histories had, and not just because of the contents. The pages of the book were worn and stained from constant turning. Ashravan *had* written this book to be read—by himself.

58

What memories had Ashravan sought so profoundly that he would read this book over and over and over again? Was he vain, enjoying the thrill of past conquests? Was he, instead, insecure? Did he spend hours searching these words because he wanted to justify his mistakes? Or was there another reason?

The door to her chambers opened. They had stopped knocking. Why would they? They already denied her any semblance of privacy. She was still a captive, just a more important one than before.

Arbiter Frava entered, graceful and long faced, wearing robes of a soft violet. Her grey braid was spun with gold and violet this time. Captain Zu guarded her. Inwardly, Shai sighed, adjusting her spectacles. She had been anticipating a night of study and planning, uninterrupted now that Gaotona had gone to join the festivities.

"I am told," Frava said, "that you are progressing at an unremarkable pace."

Shai set down the book. "Actually, this is quick. I am nearly ready to begin crafting stamps. As I reminded Arbiter Gaotona earlier today, I do still need a test subject who knew the emperor. The connection between them will allow me to test stamps on him, and they will stick briefly—long enough for me to try out a few things."

"One will be provided," Frava replied, walking along the table with its glistening surface. She ran a finger across it, then stopped at the red seal mark. The arbiter prodded at it. "Such an eyesore. After going to such trouble to make the table more beautiful, why not put the seal on the bottom?"

"I'm proud of my work," Shai said. "Any Forger who sees this can inspect it and see what I've done."

Frava sniffed. "You should not be proud of something like this, little thief. Besides, isn't the point of what you do to *hide* the fact that you've done it?"

"Sometimes," Shai said. "When I imitate a signature or counterfeit a painting, the subterfuge is part of the act. But with Forgery, true Forgery, you cannot hide what you've done. The stamp will always be there, describing exactly what has happened. You might as well be proud of it."

It was the odd conundrum of her life. To be a Forger was not just about soulstamps—it was about the art of mimicry in its entirety. Writing, art, personal signets . . . an apprentice Forger—mentored half in secret by her people—learned all mundane forgery before being taught to use soulstamps.

The stamps were the highest order of their art, but they were the most difficult to hide. Yes, a seal could be placed in an out-of-the way place on an object, then covered over. Shai had done that very thing on occasion. However, so long as the seal was somewhere to be found, a Forgery could not be perfect.

"Leave us," Frava said to Zu and the guards.

"But—" Zu said, stepping forward.

"I do not like to repeat myself, Captain," Frava said.

Zu growled softly, but bowed in obedience. He gave Shai a glare—that was practically a second occupation for him, these days—and retreated with his men. They shut the door with a click.

The Bloodsealer's stamp still hung there on the door, renewed this morning. The Bloodsealer came at the same time most days. Shai had kept specific notes. On days when he was a little late, his seal started to dim right before he arrived. He always got to her in time to renew it, but perhaps someday . . .

Frava inspected Shai, eyes calculating.

Shai met that gaze with a steady one of her own. "Zu assumes I'm going to do something horrible to you while we're alone."

"Zu is simpleminded," Frava said, "though he is very useful when someone needs to be killed. Hopefully you won't ever have to experience his efficiency firsthand."

"You're not worried?" Shai said. "You are alone in a room with a monster."

"I'm alone in a room with an opportunist," Frava said, strolling to the door and inspecting the seal burning there. "You won't harm me. You're too curious about why I sent the guards away."

Actually, Shai thought, *I know precisely why you sent them away. And why you came to me during a time when all of your associate arbiters were guaranteed to be busy at the festival.* She waited for Frava to make the offer.

"Has it occurred to you," Frava said, "how . . . useful to the empire it would be to have an emperor who listened to a voice of wisdom when it spoke to him?"

"Surely Emperor Ashravan already did that."

"On occasion," Frava said. "On other occasions, he could be . . . belligerently foolish. Wouldn't it be amazing if, upon his rebirth, he were found lacking that tendency?"

"I thought you wanted him to act exactly like he used to," Shai said. "As close to the real thing as possible."

"True, true. But you are renowned as one of the greatest Forgers ever to live, and I have it on good authority that you are specifically talented with stamping your own soul. Surely you can replicate dear Ashravan's soul with authenticity, yet also make him inclined to listen to reason . . . when that reason is spoken by specific individuals."

Nights afire, Shai thought. *You're willing to just come out and say it, aren't you? You want me to build a back door into the emperor's soul, and you don't even have the decency to feel ashamed about that.*

"I . . . might be able to do such a thing," Shai said, as if considering it for the first time. "It would be difficult. I'd need a reward worth the effort."

"A suitable reward *would* be appropriate," Frava said, turning to her. "I realize you were probably planning to leave the Imperial Seat following your release, but why? This city could be a place of great opportunity to you, with a sympathetic ruler on the throne."

"Be more blunt, Arbiter," Shai said. "I have a long night ahead of me studying while others celebrate. I don't have the mind for word games."

"The city has a thriving clandestine smuggling trade," Frava said. "Keeping track of it has been a hobby of mine. It would serve me to have someone proper running it. I will give it to you, should you do this task for me."

That was always their mistake—assuming they knew why Shai did what she did. Assuming she'd jump at a chance like this, assuming that a smuggler and a Forger were basically the same thing because they both disobeyed someone else's laws.

"That sounds pleasant," Shai said, smiling her most genuine smile—the one that had an edge of overt deceptiveness to it.

Frava smiled deeply in return. "I will leave you to consider," she said, pulling open the door and clapping for the guards to reenter.

Shai sank down into her chair, horrified. Not because of the offer—she'd been expecting one like it for days now—but because she had only now understood the implications. The offer of the smuggling trade was, of course, false. Frava might have been able to deliver such a thing, but she wouldn't. Even assuming that the woman hadn't already been planning to have Shai killed, this offer sealed that eventuality.

There was more to it, though. Far more. *So far as she knows, she just planted in my head the idea of building control into the emperor. She won't trust my Forgery. She'll be expecting me to put in back doors of my own, ones that give* me *and not her complete control over Ashravan.*

What did that mean?

It meant that Frava had another Forger standing by. One, likely, without the talent or the bravado to try Forging someone else's soul—but one who could look over Shai's work and find any back doors she put in. This Forger would be better trusted, and could rewrite Shai's work to put Frava in control.

They might even be able to finish Shai's work, if she got it far enough along first. Shai had intended to use the full hundred days to plan her escape, but now she realized that her sudden extermination could come at any time.

The closer she got to finishing the project, the more likely that grew.

Day Thirty

"THIS IS NEW," Gaotona said, inspecting the stained glass window.

That had been a particularly pleasing bit of inspiration on Shai's part. Attempts to Forge the window to a better version of itself had repeatedly failed; each time, after five minutes or so, the window had reverted to its cracked, gap-sided self.

Then Shai had found a bit of colored glass rammed into one side of the frame. The window, she realized, had once been a stained glass piece, like many in the palace. It had been broken, and whatever had shattered the window had also bent the frame, producing those gaps that let in the frigid breeze.

Rather than repairing it as it had been meant to be, someone had put ordinary glass into the window and left it to crack. A stamp from Shai in the bottom right corner had restored the window, rewriting its history so that a caring master craftsman had discovered the fallen window and remade it. That seal had taken immediately. Even after all this time, the window had seen itself as something beautiful.

Or maybe she was just getting romantic again.

"You said you would bring me a test subject today," Shai said, blowing the dust off the end of a freshly carved soulstamp. She engraved a series of quick marks on the back—the side opposite the elaborately carved front. The setting mark finished every soulstamp, indicating no more carving was to come. Shai had always fancied it to look like the shape of MaiPon, her homeland.

Those marks finished, she held the stamp over a flame. This was a property of soulstone; fire hardened it, so it could not be chipped. She didn't need to take this step. The anchoring marks on the top were all it really needed, and she could carve a stamp out of anything, really, so long as the carving was precise. Soulstone was prized, however, because of this hardening process.

Once the entire thing was blackened from the candle's flame—first one end, then the other—she held it up and blew on it strongly. Flakes of char blew free with her breath, revealing the beautiful red and grey marbled stone beneath.

"Yes," Gaotona said. "A test subject. I brought one, as promised." Gaotona crossed the small room toward the door, where Zu stood guard.

Shai leaned back in her chair, which she'd Forged

into something far more comfortable a couple of days back, and waited. She had made a bet with herself. Would the subject be one of the emperor's guards? Or would it be some lowly palace functionary, perhaps the man who took notes for Ashravan? Which person would the arbiters force to endure Shai's blasphemy in the name of a supposedly greater good?

Gaotona sat down in the chair by the door.

"Well?" Shai asked.

He raised his hands to the sides. "You may begin."

Shai dropped her feet to the ground, sitting up straight. "You?"

"Yes."

"You're one of the arbiters! One of the most powerful people in the empire!"

"Ah," he said. "I had not noticed. I fit your specifications. I am male, was born in Ashravan's own birthplace, and I knew him very well."

"But . . ." Shai trailed off.

Gaotona leaned forward, clasping his hands. "We debated this for weeks. Other options were offered, but it was determined that we could not in good conscience order one of our people to undergo this blasphemy. The only conclusion was to offer up one of ourselves."

Shai shook herself free of shock. *Frava would have had no trouble ordering someone else to this,* she thought. *Nor would the others. You must have insisted upon this, Gaotona.*

They considered him a rival; they were probably happy to let him fall to Shai's supposedly horrible, twisted acts. What she planned was perfectly harmless, but there was no way she'd convince a Grand of that. Still, she found herself wishing she could put Gaotona at ease as she pulled her chair up beside him and opened the small box of stamps she had crafted over the past three weeks.

"These stamps will not take," she said, holding up one of them. "That is a Forger's term for a stamp that makes a change that is too unnatural to be stable. I doubt any of these will affect you for longer than a minute—and that's assuming I did them correctly."

Gaotona hesitated, then nodded.

"The human soul is different from that of an object," Shai continued. "A person is constantly growing, changing, shifting. That makes a soulstamp used on a person wear out in a way that doesn't happen with objects. Even in the best of cases, a soulstamp used on a person lasts only a day. My Essence Marks are an example. After about twenty-six hours, they fade away."

"So . . . the emperor?"

"If I do my job well," Shai said, "he will need to be stamped each morning, much as the Bloodsealer stamps my door. I will fashion into the seal, however, the capacity for him to remember, grow, and learn—he won't revert back to the same state each morning, and will be able to build upon the foundation I give him. However, much as a human body wears down and needs sleep, a soulstamp on one of us must be reset. Fortunately, anyone can do the stamping—Ashravan himself should be able to—once the stamp itself is prepared correctly."

She gave Gaotona the stamp she held, letting him inspect it.

"Each of the particular stamps I will use today," she continued, "will change something small about your past or your innate personality. As you are not Ashravan, the changes will not take. However, you two are similar enough in history that the seals should last for a short time, if I've done them well."

"You mean this is a . . . pattern for the emperor's soul?" Gaotona asked, looking over the stamp.

"No. Just a Forgery of a small part of it. I'm not even sure if the final product will work. So far as I know, no one has ever tried something exactly like this before. But there are accounts of people Forging someone else's soul for . . . nefarious purposes. I'm drawing on that knowledge to accomplish this. From what I know, if these seals last for at least a minute on you, they should last far longer on the emperor, as they are attuned to his specific past."

"A small piece of his soul," Gaotona said, handing back the seal. "So these tests . . . you will not use these seals in the final product?"

"No, but I'll take the patterns that work and incorporate them into a greater fabrication. Think of these seals as single characters in a large scroll; once I am done, I'll be able to put them together and tell a story. The story of a man's history and personality. Unfortunately, even if the Forgery takes, there will be small differences. I suggest that you begin spreading rumors that the emperor was wounded. Not terribly, mind you, but imply a good knock to the head. That will explain discrepancies."

"There are already rumors of his death," Gaotona said, "spread by the Glory Faction."

"Well, indicate he was wounded instead."

"But—"

Shai raised the stamp. "Even if I accomplish the impossible—which, mind you, I've done only on rare occasions—the Forgery will not have all of the emperor's memories. It can only contain things I have been able to read about or guess. Ashravan will have had many private conversations that the Forgery will *not* be able to recall. I can imbue him with a keen ability to fake—I have a particular understanding of that sort of thing—but fakery can only take a person so far. Eventually, someone will realize that he has large holes in his memory. Spread the rumors, Gaotona. You're going to need them."

He nodded, then pulled back his sleeve to expose his arm for her to stamp. She raised the stamp, and

Gaotona sighed, then squeezed his eyes shut and nodded again.

She pressed it against his skin. As always, when the stamp touched the skin, it felt as if she were pressing it against something rigid—as if his arm had become stone. The stamp *sank in* slightly. That made for a disconcerting sensation when working on a person. She rotated the stamp, then pulled it back, leaving a red seal on Gaotona's arm. She took out her pocket watch, observing the ticking hand.

The seal gave off faint wisps of red smoke; that happened only when living things were stamped. The soul fought against the rewriting. The seal didn't puff away immediately, though. Shai released a held breath. That was a good sign.

She wondered . . . if she were to try something like this on the emperor, would his soul fight against the invasion? Or instead, would it accept the stamp, wishing to have righted what had gone wrong? Much as that window had wanted to be restored to its former beauty. She didn't know.

Gaotona opened his eyes. "Did it . . . work?"

"It took, for now," Shai said.

"I don't feel any different."

"That is the point. If the emperor could *feel* the stamp's effects, he would realize that something was wrong. Now, answer me without thought; speak by instinct only. What is your favorite color?"

"Green," he said immediately.

"Why?"

"Because . . ." He trailed off, cocking his head. "Because it is."

"And your brother?"

"I hardly remember him," Gaotona said with a shrug. "He died when I was very young."

"It is good he did," Shai said. "He would have made a terrible emperor, if he had been chosen in—"

Gaotona stood up. "Don't you dare speak ill of him! I will have you . . ." He stiffened, glancing at Zu, who had reached for his sword in alarm. "I . . . Brother . . . ?"

The seal faded away.

"A minute and five seconds," Shai said. "That one looks good."

Gaotona raised a hand to his head. "I can remember having a brother. But . . . I don't have one, and never have. I can remember idolizing him; I can remember pain when he died. Such *pain* . . ."

"That will fade," Shai said. "The impressions will wash away like the remnants of a bad dream. In an hour, you'll barely be able to recall what it was that upset you." She scribbled some notes. "I think you reacted too strongly to me insulting your brother's memory. Ashravan worshipped his brother, but kept his feelings buried deep out of guilt that perhaps his brother would have made a better emperor than he."

"What? Are you sure?"

"About this?" Shai said. "Yes. I'll have to revise that stamp a little bit, but I think it is mostly right."

Gaotona sat back down, regarding her with ancient eyes that seemed to be trying to pierce her, to dig deep inside. "You know a great deal about people."

"It's one of the early steps of our training," Shai said. "Before we're even allowed to *touch* soulstone."

"Such potential . . ." Gaotona whispered.

Shai forced down an immediate burst of annoyance. How dare he look at her like that, as if she were wasting her life? She loved Forgery. The thrill, a life spent getting ahead by her wits. That was what she *was*. Wasn't it?

She thought of one specific Essence Mark, locked away with the others. It was one Mark she had never used, yet was at the same time the most precious of the five.

"Let's try another," Shai said, ignoring those eyes of Gaotona's. She couldn't afford to grow offended. Aunt Sol had always said that pride would be Shai's greatest danger in life.

"Very well," Gaotona said, "but I am confused at one thing. From what little you've told me of this process, I cannot fathom why these seals even begin to work on me. Don't you need to know a thing's history exactly to make a seal work on it?"

"To make them stick, yes," Shai said. "As I've said, it's about plausibility."

"But this is completely implausible! I don't have a brother."

"Ah. Well, let me see if I can explain," she said, settling back. "I am rewriting your soul to match that of the emperor—just as I rewrote the history of that window to include new stained glass. In both cases, it works because of *familiarity*. The window frame knows what a stained glass window should look like. It once had stained glass in it. Even though the new window is not the same as the one it once held, the seal works because the general concept of a stained glass window has been fulfilled.

"You spent a great deal of time around the emperor. Your soul is familiar with his, much as the window frame is familiar with the stained glass. This is why I have to try out the seals on someone like you, and not on myself. When I stamp you, it's like . . . it's like I'm presenting to your soul a piece of something it should know. It only works if the piece is very small, but so long as it is—and so long as the soul considers the piece a familiar part of Ashravan, as I've indicated—the stamp will take for a brief time before being rejected."

Gaotona regarded her with bemusement.

"Sounds like superstitious nonsense to you, I assume?" Shai said.

"It is . . . rather mystical," Gaotona said, spreading his hands before him. "A window frame knowing the 'concept' of a stained glass window? A soul understanding the concept of another soul?"

"These things exist beyond us," Shai said, preparing another seal. "We think about windows, we know about windows; what is and isn't a window takes on . . . meaning, in the Spiritual Realm. Takes on life, after a fashion. Believe the explanation or do not; I guess it doesn't matter. The fact is that I can try these seals on you, and if they stick for at least a minute, it's a very good indication that I've hit on something.

"Ideally, I'd try this on the emperor himself, but in his state, he would not be able to answer my questions. I need to not only get these to take, but I need to make them work together—and that will require your explanations of what you are feeling so I can nudge the design in the right directions. Now, your arm again, please?"

"Very well." Gaotona composed himself, and Shai pressed another seal against his arm. She locked it with a half turn, but as soon as she pulled the stamp away, the seal vanished in a puff of red.

"Blast," Shai said.

"What happened?" Gaotona said, reaching fingers to his arm. He smeared mundane ink; the seal had vanished so quickly, the ink hadn't even been incorporated into its workings. "What have you done to me this time?"

"Nothing, it appears," Shai said, inspecting the head

of the stamp for flaws. She found none. "I had *that* one wrong. Very wrong."

"What was it?"

"The reason Ashravan agreed to become emperor," Shai said. "Nights afire. I was certain I had this one." She shook her head, setting the stamp aside. Ashravan, it appeared, had not stepped up to offer himself as emperor because of a deep-seated desire to prove himself to his family and to escape the distant—but long—shadow of his brother.

"I can tell you why he did it, Forger," Gaotona said.

She eyed him. *This man encouraged Ashravan to step toward the imperial throne,* she thought. Ashravan eventually hated him for it. *I think.*

"All right," she said. "Why?"

"He wanted to change things," Gaotona said. "In the empire."

"He doesn't speak of this in his journal."

"Ashravan was a humble man."

Shai raised an eyebrow. That didn't match the reports she'd been given.

"Oh, he had a temper," Gaotona said. "And if you got him arguing, he would sink his teeth in and hold fast to his point. But the man . . . the man he was . . . Deep down, that was a humble man. You will have to understand this about him."

"I see," she said. *You did it to him too, didn't you?* Shai thought. *That look of disappointment, that implication we should be better people than we are.* Shai wasn't the only one who felt that Gaotona regarded her as if he were a displeased grandfather.

That made her want to dismiss the man as irrelevant. Except . . . he had offered himself to her tests. He thought what she did was horrible, so he insisted on taking the punishment himself, instead of sending another.

You're genuine, aren't you, old man? Shai thought as Gaotona sat back, eyes distant as he considered the emperor. She found herself displeased.

In her business, there were many who laughed at honest men, calling them easy pickings. That was a fallacy. Being honest did not make one naive. A dishonest fool and an honest fool were equally easy to scam; you just went about it in different ways.

However, a man who was honest and clever was always, *always* more difficult to scam than someone who was both dishonest and clever.

Sincerity. It was so difficult, by definition, to fake.

"What are you thinking behind those eyes of yours?" Gaotona asked, leaning forward.

"I was thinking that you must have treated the emperor as you did me, annoying him with constant nagging about what he should accomplish."

Gaotona snorted. "I probably did just that. It does not mean my points are, or were, incorrect. He could have . . . well, he could have become more than he did. Just as you *could* become a marvelous artist."

"I am one."

"A real one."

"I am one."

Gaotona shook his head. "Frava's painting . . . there is something we are missing about it, isn't there? She had the forgery inspected, and the assessors found a few tiny mistakes. I couldn't see them without help—but they are there. Upon reflection, they seem odd to me. The strokes are impeccable, masterful even. The style is a perfect match. If you could manage that, why would you have made such errors as putting the moon too low? It's a subtle mistake, but it occurs to me that you would never have made such an error—not unintentionally, at least."

Shai turned to get another seal.

"The painting they think is the original," Gaotona said, "the one hanging in Frava's office right now . . . It's a fake too, isn't it?"

"Yes," Shai admitted with a sigh. "I swapped the paintings a few days before trying for the scepter; I was investigating palace security. I sneaked into the gallery, entered Frava's offices, and made the change as a test."

"So the one they assume is fake, *it* must be the original," Gaotona said, smiling. "You painted those mistakes *over* the original to make it seem like it was a replica!"

"Actually, no," Shai said. "Though I have used that trick in the past. They're both fakes. One is simply the obvious fake, planted to be discovered in case something went wrong."

"So the original is still hidden somewhere . . ." Gaotona said, sounding curious. "You sneaked into the palace to investigate security, then you replaced the original painting with a copy. You left a second, slightly worse copy in your room as a false trail. If you were found out while sneaking in—or if you were for some reason sold out by an ally—we would search your room and find the poor copy, and assume that you hadn't yet accomplished your swap. The officers would take the good copy and believe it to be authentic. That way, no one would keep looking for the original."

"More or less."

"That's very clever," Gaotona said. "Why, if you were captured sneaking into the palace trying to steal the scepter, you could confess that you were trying to steal only the painting. A search of your room would turn up the fake, and you'd be charged with attempted theft from an individual, in this case Frava, which is a much lesser crime than trying to steal an imperial relic. You would get ten years of labor instead of a death sentence."

"Unfortunately," Shai said, "I was betrayed at the wrong moment. The Fool arranged for me to be caught after I'd left the gallery with the scepter."

"But what of the original painting? Where did you hide it?" He hesitated. "It's still in the palace, isn't it?"

"After a fashion."

Gaotona looked at her, still smiling.

"I burned it," Shai said.

The smile vanished immediately. "You lie."

"Not this time, old man," Shai said. "The painting wasn't worth the risk to get it out of the gallery. I only pulled that swap to test security. I got the fake in easily; people aren't searched going in, only coming out. The scepter was my true goal. Stealing the painting was secondary. After I replaced it, I tossed the original into one of the main gallery hearths."

"That's *horrible*," Gaotona said. "It was an original ShuXen, his greatest masterpiece! He's gone blind, and can no longer paint. Do you realize the cost . . ." He sputtered. "I don't understand. Why, *why* would you do something like that?"

"It doesn't matter. No one will know what I've done. They will keep looking at the fake and be satisfied, so there's no harm done."

"That painting was a priceless work of art!" Gaotona glared at her. "Your swap of it was about pride and nothing else. You didn't care about selling the original. You just wanted your copy hanging in the gallery instead. You destroyed something wonderful so that you could elevate yourself!"

She shrugged. There was more to the story, but the fact was, she *had* burned the painting. She had her reasons.

"We are done for the day," Gaotona said, red faced.

He waved a hand at her, dismissive as he stood up. "I had begun to think . . . Bah!"

He stalked out the door.

Day Forty-Two

EACH PERSON was a puzzle.

That was how Tao, her first trainer in Forgery, had explained it. A Forger wasn't a simple scam artist or trickster. A Forger was an artist who painted with human perception.

Any grime-covered urchin on the street could scam someone. A Forger sought loftier heights. Common scammers worked by pulling a cloth over someone's eyes, then fleeing before realization hit. A Forger had to create something so perfect, so beautiful, so *real* that their subjects never questioned.

A person was like a dense forest thicket, overgrown with a twisting mess of vines, weeds, shrubs, saplings, and flowers. No person was one single emotion; no person had only one desire. They had many, and usually those desires conflicted with one another like two rosebushes fighting for the same patch of ground.

Respect the people you lie to, Tao had taught her. Steal from them long enough, and you will begin to understand them.

Shai crafted a book as she worked, a true history of Emperor Ashravan's life. It would become a truer history than those his scribes had written to glorify him, a truer history even than the one written by his own hand. Shai slowly pieced together the puzzle, crawling into the thicket that had been Ashravan's mind.

He *had* been idealistic, as Gaotona said. She saw it now in the cautious worry of his early writings and in the way he had treated his servants. The empire was not a terrible thing. Neither was it a wonderful thing. The empire simply *was*. The people suffered its rule because they were comfortable with its little tyrannies. Corruption was inevitable. You lived with it. It was either that or accept the chaos of the unknown.

Grands were treated with extreme favoritism. Entering government service, the most lucrative and prestigious of occupations, was often more about bribes and connections than it was about skill or aptitude. In addition, some of those who best served the empire— merchants and laborers—were systematically robbed by a hundred hands in their pockets.

Everyone knew these things. Ashravan had wanted to change them. At first.

And then . . . Well, there hadn't been a specific *and*

then. Poets would point to a single flaw in Ashravan's nature that had led him to failure, but a person was no more one flaw than they were one passion. If Shai based her Forgery on any single attribute, she would create a mockery, not a man.

But . . . was that the best she could hope for? Perhaps she should try for authenticity in one specific setting, making an emperor who could act properly in court, but could not fool those closest to him. Perhaps that would work well enough, like the stage props from a playhouse. Those served their purpose while the play was going, but failed serious inspection.

That was an achievable goal. Perhaps she should go to the arbiters, explain what was possible, and give them a lesser emperor—a puppet they could use at official functions, then whisk away with explanations that he was growing sickly.

She could do that.

She found that she didn't want to.

That wasn't the challenge. That was the street thief's version of a scam, intended for short-term gain. The Forger's way was to create something enduring.

Deep down, she was thrilled by the challenge. She found that she *wanted* to make Ashravan live. She wanted to try, at least.

Shai lay back on her bed, which by now she had Forged to something more comfortable, with posts and a deep comforter. She kept the curtains drawn. Her guards for the evening played a round of cards at her table.

Why do you care about making Ashravan live? Shai thought to herself. *The arbiters will kill you before you can even see if this works. Escape should be your only goal.*

And yet . . . the *emperor* himself. She had chosen to steal the Moon Scepter because it was the most famous piece in the empire. She had wanted one of her works to be on display in the grand Imperial Gallery.

This task she now worked on, however . . . this was something far greater. What Forger had accomplished such a feat? A Forgery, sitting on the Rose Throne *itself?*

No, she told herself, more forceful this time. *Don't be lured. Pride, Shai. Don't let the pride drive you.*

She opened her book to the back pages, where she'd hidden her escape plans in a cypher, disguised to look like a dictionary of terms and people.

That Bloodsealer had come in running the other day, as if frightened that he'd be late to reset his seal. His clothing had smelled of strong drink. He was enjoying the palace's hospitality. If she could make him come early one morning, then ensure that he got extra drunk that night . . .

The mountains of the Strikers bordered Dzhamar, where the swamps of the Bloodsealers were located. Their hatred of one another ran deep, perhaps deeper than their loyalty to the empire. Several of the Strikers in particular seemed revolted when the Bloodsealer came. Shai had begun befriending those guards. Jokes in passing. Mentions of a coincidental similarity in her background and theirs. The Strikers weren't supposed to talk to Shai, but weeks had passed without Shai doing anything more than poring through books and chatting with old arbiters. The guards were bored, and boredom made people easy to manipulate.

Shai had access to plenty of soulstone, and she would use it. However, often more elementary methods were of greater use. People always expected a Forger to use seals for everything. Grands told stories of dark witchcraft, of Forgers placing seals on a person's feet while they slept, changing their personalities. Invading them, raping their minds.

The truth was that a soulstamp was often a Forger's last resort. It was too easy to detect. *Not that I wouldn't give my right hand for my Essence Marks right now . . .*

Almost, she was tempted to try carving a new Mark to use in getting away. They'd be expecting that, however, and she would have real trouble performing the hundreds of tests she'd need to do to make one work. Testing on her own arm would be reported by the guards, and testing on Gaotona would never work.

And using an Essence Mark she hadn't tested . . . well, that could go very, very poorly. No, her plans for escape would use soulstamps, but their heart would involve more traditional methods of subterfuge.

Day Fifty-Eight

SHAI WAS READY when Frava next visited.

The woman paused in the doorway, the guards shuffling out without objection as Captain Zu took their place. "You've been busy," Frava noted.

Shai looked up from her research. Frava wasn't referring to her progress, but to the room. Most recently, Shai had improved the floor. It hadn't been difficult. The rock used to build the palace—the quarry, the dates, the stonemasons—all were matters of historic record.

"You like it?" Shai asked. "The marble works well with the hearth, I think."

Frava turned, then blinked. "A *hearth?* Where did you . . . Is this room bigger than it was?"

"The storage room next door wasn't being used," Shai mumbled, turning back to her book. "And the division between these two rooms was recent, constructed only a few years back. I rewrote the construction so that this room was made the larger of the two, and so that a hearth was installed."

Frava seemed stunned. "I wouldn't have thought . . ." The woman looked back to Shai, and her face adopted its usual severe mask. "I find it difficult to believe that you are taking your duty seriously, Forger. You are here to make an emperor, not remodel the palace."

"Carving soulstone relaxes me," Shai said. "As does having a workspace that doesn't remind me of a closet. You will have your emperor's soul in time, Frava."

The arbiter stalked through the room, inspecting the desk. "Then you have begun the emperor's soulstone?"

"I've begun many of them," Shai said. "It will be a complex process. I've tested well over a hundred stamps on Gaotona—"

"*Arbiter* Gaotona."

"—on the old man. Each is only a tiny slice of the puzzle. Once I have all of the pieces working, I'll recarve them in smaller, more delicate etchings. That will allow me to combine about a dozen test stamps into one final stamp."

"But you said you'd tested over a hundred," Frava said, frowning. "You'll only use twelve of those in the end?"

Shai laughed. "Twelve? To Forge an entire *soul?* Hardly. The final stamp, the one you will need to use on the emperor each morning, will be like . . . a linchpin, or the keystone of an arch. It will be the only one that will need to be placed on his skin, but it will connect a lattice of hundreds of other stamps."

Shai reached to the side, taking out her book of notes, including initial sketches of the final stamps. "I'll take these and stamp them onto a metal plate, then link that to the stamp you will place on Ashravan each day. He'll need to keep the plate close at all times."

"He'll need to carry a metal plate with him," Frava said drily, "*and* he will need to be stamped each day? This will make it difficult for the man to live a normal life, don't you think?"

"Being emperor makes it difficult for any man to live a normal life, I suspect. You will make it work. It's customary for the plate to be designed as a piece of adornment. A large medallion, perhaps, or an upper arm bracer with square sides. If you look at my own Essence Marks, you'll notice they were done in the same way, and that the box contains a plate for each one." Shai hesitated. "That said, I've never done this exact thing before; no one has. There is a chance . . . and I'd say a fair one . . . that over time, the emperor's brain will absorb the information. Like . . . like if you traced the exact same image on a stack of papers every day for a year, at the end the layers below will contain the image as well. Perhaps after a few years of being stamped, he won't need the treatment any longer."

"I still name it egregious."

"Worse than being dead?" Shai asked.

Frava rested her hand on Shai's book of notes and half-finished sketches. Then she picked it up. "I will have our scribes copy this."

Shai stood up. "I need it."

"I'm sure you do," Frava said. "That is precisely why it should be copied, just in case."

"Copying it will take too long."

"I will have it back to you in a day," Frava said lightly, stepping away. Shai reached for her, and Captain Zu stepped up, sword already half out of its sheath.

Frava turned to him. "Now, now, Captain. That won't be needed. The Forger is protective of her work. That is good. It shows that she is invested."

Shai and Zu locked gazes. *He wants me dead,* Shai thought. *Badly.* She'd figured him out by now. Guarding the palace was his duty, one that Shai had invaded by her theft. Zu hadn't captured her; the Imperial Fool had turned her in. Zu felt insecure because of his failure, and so he wanted to remove Shai in retribution.

Shai eventually broke his gaze. Though it galled her, she needed to take the submissive side of this interaction. "Be careful," she warned Frava. "Do not let them lose even a single page."

"I will protect this as if . . . as if the emperor's life depended on it." Frava found her joke amusing, and she gave Shai a rare smile. "You have considered the other matter we discussed?"

"Yes."

"And?"

"Yes."

Frava's smile deepened. "We will talk again soon."

Frava left with the book, nearly two months' worth of work. Shai knew exactly what the woman was up to. Frava wasn't going to have it copied—she was going to show it to her other Forger and see if it was far enough along for him to finish the job.

If he determined that it was, Shai would be executed, quietly, before the other arbiters could object. Zu would likely do it himself. It could all end here.

Day Fifty-Nine

SHAI SLEPT POORLY that night.

She was certain that her preparations had been thorough. And yet now, she had to wait as if with a noose around her neck. It made her anxious. What if she'd misread the situation?

She had made her notations in the book intentionally opaque, each of them a subtle indication of just how *enormous* this project was. The cramped writing, the numerous cross-references, the lists and lists of reminders to herself of things to do . . . Each of these would work together with the thick book as a whole to indicate that her work was mind-breakingly complex.

It was a forgery. One of the most difficult types—a forgery that did not imitate a specific person or object. This was a forgery of *tone*.

Stay away, the tone of that book said. *You don't want to try to finish this. You want to let Shai continue to do the*

*hard parts, because the work required to do it yourself would
be enormous. And . . . if you fail . . . it will be your head on
the line.*

That book was one of the most subtle forgeries she'd
ever created. Each word in it was true and yet a lie at
the same time. Only a master Forger might see through
it, might notice how hard she was working to illustrate
the danger and difficulty of the project.

How skilled was Frava's Forger?

Would Shai be dead before morning?

She didn't sleep. She wanted to and she should
have. Waiting out the hours, minutes, and seconds was
excruciating. The thought of lying in bed asleep when
they came for her . . . that was worse.

Eventually, she got up and retrieved some accounts
of Ashravan's life. The guards playing cards at her table
gave her a glance. One even nodded with sympathy at
her red eyes and tired posture. "Light too bright?" he
asked, gesturing at the lamp.

"No," Shai said. "Just a thought in my brain that
won't get out."

She spent the night in bed pouring herself into
Ashravan's life. Frustrated to be lacking her notes, she
got out a fresh sheet and began some new ones she'd
add to her book when it returned. If it did.

She felt that she finally understood why Ashravan
had abandoned his youthful optimism. At least, she
knew the factors that had combined to lead him down

that path. Corruption was part of it, but not the main part. Again, lack of self-confidence contributed, but hadn't been the decisive factor.

No, Ashravan's downfall had been life itself. Life in the palace, life as part of an empire that clicked along like a clock. Everything worked. Oh, it didn't work as well as it might. But it *did* work.

Challenging that took effort, and effort was sometimes hard to muster. He had lived a life of leisure. Ashravan hadn't been lazy, but it didn't require laziness to be swept up in the workings of imperial bureaucracy—to tell yourself that next month you'd go and demand that your changes be made. Over time, it had become easier and easier to float along the course of the great river that was the Rose Empire.

In the end, he'd grown indulgent. He'd focused more on the beauty of his palace than on the lives of his subjects. He had allowed the arbiters to handle more and more government functions.

Shai sighed. Even that description of him was too simplistic. It neglected to mention *who* the emperor had been, and who he had become. A chronology of events didn't speak of his temper, his fondness for debate, his eye for beauty, or his habit of writing terrible, *terrible* poetry and then expecting all who served him to tell him how wonderful it was.

It also didn't speak of his arrogance, or his secret wish that he could have been something else. That was why he had gone back over his book again and again. Perhaps he had been looking for that branching point in his life where he had stepped down the wrong path.

He hadn't understood. There was rarely an obvious branching point in a person's life. People changed slowly, over time. You didn't take one step, then find yourself in a completely new location. You first took a little step off a path to avoid some rocks. For a while, you walked alongside the path, but then you wandered out a little way to step on softer soil. Then you stopped paying attention as you drifted farther and farther away. Finally, you found yourself in the wrong city, wondering why the signs on the roadway hadn't led you better.

The door to her room opened.

Shai bolted upright in her bed, nearly dropping her notes. They'd come for her.

But . . . no, it was *morning* already. Light trickled through the stained glass window, and the guards were standing up and stretching. The one who had opened the door was the Bloodsealer. He looked hungover again, and carried a stack of papers in his hand, as he often did.

He's early this morning, Shai thought, checking her pocket watch. *Why early today, when he's late so often?*

The Bloodsealer cut her and stamped the door without a word, causing the pain to burn in Shai's arm. He hurried out of the room, as if off to some appointment. Shai stared after him, then shook her head.

A moment later, the door opened again and Frava entered.

"Oh, you're up," the woman said as the Strikers saluted her. Frava set Shai's book down on the table with a thump. She seemed annoyed. "The scribes are done. Get back to work."

Frava left in a bustle. Shai leaned back in her bed, sighing in relief. Her ruse had worked. That should earn her a few more weeks.

Day Seventy

"SO THIS SYMBOL," Gaotona said, pointing at one of her sketches of the greater stamps she would soon carve, "is a time notation, indicating a moment specifically . . . seven years ago?"

"Yes," Shai said, dusting off the end of a freshly carved soulstamp. "You learn quickly."

"I am undergoing surgery each day, so to speak," Gaotona said. "It makes me more comfortable to know the kinds of knives being used."

"The changes aren't—"

"Aren't permanent," he said. "Yes, so you keep saying." He stretched out his arm for her to stamp. "However, it makes me wonder. One can cut the body, and it will heal—but do it over and over again in the same spot, and you *will* scar. The soul cannot be so different."

"Except, of course, that it's *completely* different," Shai said, stamping his arm.

He had never quite forgiven her for what she had done in burning ShuXen's masterpiece. She could see it in him, when they interacted. He was no longer just disappointed in her, he was angry at her.

Anger faded with time, and they had a functional working relationship again.

Gaotona cocked his head. "I . . . Now *that* is odd."

"Odd in what way?" Shai asked, watching the seconds pass on her pocket watch.

"I remember encouraging *myself* to become emperor. And . . . and I resent myself. For . . . mother of light, is that really how he regarded me?"

The seal remained in place for fifty-seven seconds. Good enough. "Yes," she said as the seal faded away. "I believe that is exactly how he regarded you." She felt a thrill. *Finally* that seal had worked!

She was getting close now. Close to understanding the emperor, close to having the puzzle come together. Whenever she neared the end of a project—a painting, a large-scale soul Forgery, a sculpture—there came a moment in the process where she could *see* the entire work, even if it was far from finished. When that moment came, in her mind's eye, the work was complete; actually finishing it was almost a formality.

She was nearly there with this project. The emperor's soul spread out before her, with only some few corners still shadowed. She wanted to see it through; she *longed* to find out if she could make him live again. After reading so much about him, after coming to feel as if she knew him so well, she needed to finish.

Surely her escape could wait until then.

"That was it, wasn't it?" Gaotona asked. "That was the stamp that you've tried a dozen times without success, the seal representing why he stood up to become emperor."

"Yes," Shai said.

"His relationship with me," Gaotona said. "You made his decision depend upon his relationship with me, and . . . and the sense of shame he felt when speaking with me."

"Yes."

"And it took."

"Yes."

Gaotona sat back. "Mother of lights . . ." he whispered again.

Shai took the seal and put it with those that she had confirmed as workable.

Over the last few weeks, each of the other arbiters had done as Frava had, coming to Shai and offering her fantastic promises in exchange for giving them ultimate control of the emperor. Only Gaotona had never tried to bribe her. A genuine man, and one in the highest levels of imperial government no less. Remarkable. Using him was going to be far more difficult than she would have liked.

"I must say again," she said, turning to him, "you've

impressed me. I don't think many Grands would take the time to study soulstamps. They would eschew what they considered evil without ever trying to understand it. You've changed your mind?"

"No," Gaotona said. "I still think that what you do is, if not evil, then certainly unholy. And yet, who am I to speak? I am depending upon you to preserve us in power by means of this art we so freely call an abomination. Our hunger for power outweighs our conscience."

"True for the others," Shai said, "but that is not your personal motive."

He raised an eyebrow at her.

"You just want Ashravan back," Shai said. "You refuse to accept that you've lost him. You loved him as a son—the youth that you mentored, the emperor you always believed in, even when he didn't believe in himself."

Gaotona looked away, looking decidedly uncomfortable.

"It won't be him," Shai said. "Even if I succeed, it won't *truly* be him. You realize this, of course."

He nodded.

"But then . . . sometimes a clever Forgery is as good as the real thing," Shai said. "You are of the Heritage Faction. You surround yourself with relics that aren't truly relics, paintings that are imitations of ones long lost. I suppose having a fake relic for an emperor won't be so different. And you . . . you just want to know that you've done everything you could. For him."

"How do you do it?" Gaotona asked softly. "I've seen how you speak with the guards, how you learn even the names of the servants. You seem to know their family lives, their passions, what they do in the evenings . . . and yet you spend each day locked in this room. You haven't left it for months. How do you know these things?"

"People," Shai said, rising to fetch another seal, "by nature attempt to exercise power over what is around them. We build walls to shelter us from the wind, roofs to stop the rain. We tame the elements, bend nature to our wills. It makes us feel as if we're in control.

"Except in doing so, we merely replace one influence with another. Instead of the wind affecting us, it is a wall. A *man-made* wall. The fingers of man's influence are all about, touching everything. Man-made rugs, man-made food. Every single thing in the city that we touch, see, feel, *experience* comes as the result of some person's influence.

"We may feel in control, but we never truly are unless we understand people. Controlling our environment is no longer about blocking the wind, it's about knowing why the serving lady was crying last night, or why a particular guard always loses at cards. Or why your employer hired you in the first place."

Gaotona looked back at her as she sat, then held out

a seal to him. He hesitantly proffered an arm. "It occurs to me," he said, "that even in our extreme care not to do so, we have underestimated you, woman."

"Good," she said. "You're paying attention." She stamped him. "Now tell me, why exactly do you hate fish?"

Day Seventy-Six

I NEED TO DO IT, Shai thought as the Bloodsealer cut her arm. *Today. I could go today.*

Hidden in her other sleeve, she carried a slip of paper made to imitate the ones that the Bloodsealer often brought with him on the mornings that he came early.

She'd caught sight of a bit of wax on one of them two days back. They were letters. Realization had dawned. She'd been wrong about this man all along.

"Good news?" she asked him as he inked his stamp with her blood.

The white-lipped man gave her a sneering glance.

"From home," Shai said. "The woman you're writing, back in Dzhamar. She sent you a letter today? Post comes in the mornings here at the palace. They knock at your door, deliver a letter . . ." *And that wakes you up,* she added in her mind. *That's why you come on time those days.* "You must miss her a lot if you can't bear to leave her letter behind in your room."

The man lowered his arm and grabbed Shai by the front of her shirt. "Leave her alone, witch," he hissed. "You . . . you *leave her alone!* None of your trickery or magics!"

He was younger than she had assumed. That was a common mistake with Dzhamarians. Their white hair and skin made them seem ageless to outsiders. Shai should have known better. He was little more than a youth.

She drew her lips to a line. "You talk about *my* trickery and magics while holding in your hands a seal inked with my blood? You're the one threatening to send skeletals to hunt me, friend. All I can do is polish the odd table."

"Just . . . just . . . Ah!" The young man threw his hands up, then stamped the door.

The guards watched with nonchalant amusement and disapproval. Shai's words had been a calculated reminder that she was harmless while the Bloodsealer was the *truly* unnatural one. The guards had spent nearly three months watching her tinker about as a friendly scholar while this man drew her blood and used it for arcane horrors.

I need to drop the paper, she thought to herself, lowering her sleeve, meaning to let her forgery slip out as the guards turned away. That would put her plan into motion, her escape . . .

The real Forgery isn't finished yet. The emperor's soul.

She hesitated. Foolishly, she hesitated.

The door closed.

The opportunity passed.

Feeling numb, Shai walked to her bed and sat down on its edge, the forged letter still hidden in her sleeve. Why had she hesitated? Were her instincts for self-preservation so weak?

I can wait a little longer, she told herself. *Until Ashravan's Essence Mark is done.*

She'd been saying that for days now. Weeks, really. Each day she got closer to the deadline was another chance for Frava to strike. The woman came back with other excuses to take Shai's notes and have them inspected. They were quickly approaching the point where the other Forger wouldn't have to sort through much in order to finish Shai's work.

At least, so he would think. The further she progressed, the more impossible she realized this project was. And the more she longed to make it work anyway.

She got out her book on the emperor's life and soon found herself looking back through his youthful years. The thought of him not living again, of all of her work being merely a sham intended to distract while she planned to escape . . . those thoughts were physically *painful.*

Nights, Shai thought at herself. *You've grown fond of him. You're starting to see him like Gaotona does!* She shouldn't feel that way. She'd never met him. Besides, he was a despicable person.

But he hadn't always been. No, in truth, he hadn't ever *truly* become despicable. He had been more complex than that. Every person was. She could understand him, she could see—

"Nights!" she said, standing up and putting the book aside. She needed to clear her mind.

When Gaotona came to the room six hours later, Shai was just pressing a seal against the far wall. The elderly man opened the door and stepped in, then froze as the wall flooded with color.

Vine patterns spiraled out from Shai's stamp like sprays of paint. Green, scarlet, amber. The painting grew like something alive, leaves springing from branches, bunches of fruit exploding in succulent bursts. Thicker and thicker the pattern grew, golden trim breaking out of nothing and running like streams, rimming leaves, reflecting light.

The mural deepened, every inch imbued with an illusion of movement. Curling vines, unexpected thorns peeking from behind branches. Gaotona breathed out in awe and stepped up beside Shai. Behind, Zu stepped in, and the other two guards left and closed the door.

Gaotona reached out and felt the wall, but of course the paint was dry. So far as the wall knew, it had been painted like this years ago. Gaotona knelt down, looking at the two seals Shai put at the base of the painting. Only the third one, stamped above, had set off the transformation; the early seals were notes on how the image was to be created. Guidelines, a revision of history, instructions.

"How?" Gaotona asked.

"One of the Strikers guarded Atsuko of Jindo during his visit to the Rose Palace," Shai said. "Atsuko caught a sickness, and was stuck in his bedroom for three weeks. That was just one floor up."

"Your Forgery puts him in this room instead?"

"Yes. That was before the water damage that seeped through the ceiling last year, so it's plausible he'd have been placed here. The wall remembers Atsuko spending days too weak to leave, but having the strength for painting. A little each day, a growing pattern of vines, leaves, and berries. To pass the time."

"This shouldn't be taking," Gaotona said. "This Forgery is tenuous. You've changed too much."

"No," Shai said. "It's on the line . . . that line where the greatest beauty is found." She put the seal away. She barely remembered the last six hours. She had been caught up in the frenzy of creation.

"Still . . ." Gaotona said.

"It will take," Shai said. "If you were the wall, what would you rather be? Dreary and dull, or alive with paint?"

"Walls can't think!"

"That doesn't stop them from caring."

Gaotona shook his head, muttering about superstition. "How long?"

"To create this soulstamp? I've been etching it here and there for the last month or so. It was the last thing I wanted to do for the room."

"The artist was Jindoeese," he said. "Perhaps, because you are from the same people, it . . . But no! That's thinking like your superstition." Gaotona shook his head, trying to figure out why that painting would have taken, though it had always been obvious to Shai that this one would work.

"The Jindoeese and my people are *not* the same, by the way," Shai said testily. "We may have been related long ago, but we are completely different from them now." Grands. Just because people had similar features, Grands assumed they were practically identical.

Gaotona looked across her chamber and its fine furniture that had been carved and polished. Its marble floor with silver inlay, the crackling hearth and small chandelier. A fine rug—it had once been a bed quilt with holes in it—covered the floor. The stained glass window sparkled on the right wall, lighting the beautiful mural.

The only thing that retained its original form was the door, thick but unremarkable. She couldn't Forge that, not with that Bloodseal set into it.

"You realize that you now have the finest chamber in the palace," Gaotona said.

"I doubt that," Shai said with a sniff. "Surely the emperor's are the nicest."

"The largest, yes. Not the nicest." He knelt beside the painting, looking at her seals at the bottom. "You included detailed explanations of how this was painted."

"To create a realistic Forgery," Shai said, "you must have the technical skill you are imitating, at least to an extent."

"So you could have painted this wall yourself."

"I don't have the paints."

"But you *could* have. You could have demanded paints. I'd have given them to you. Instead, you created a Forgery."

"It's what I am," Shai said, growing annoyed at him again.

"It's what you choose to be. If a wall can desire to be a mural, Wan ShaiLu, then *you* could desire to become a great painter."

She slapped her stamp down on the table, then took a few deep breaths.

"You have a temper," Gaotona said. "Like him. Actually, I know exactly how that feels now, because you have given it to me on several occasions. I wonder if this . . . thing you do could be a tool for helping to bring awareness to people. Inscribe your emotions onto a stamp, then let others *feel* what it is to be you . . ."

"Sounds great," Shai said. "If only Forging souls weren't a horrible offense to nature."

"If only."

"If you can read those stamps, you've grown very good indeed," Shai said, pointedly changing the topic. "Almost I think you've been cheating."

"Actually . . ."

Shai perked up, banishing her anger, now that it had passed the initial flare-up. What was this?

Gaotona sheepishly reached into the deep pocket of his robe and withdrew a wooden box. The one where she kept her treasures, the five Essence Marks. Those revisions of her soul could change her, in times of need, into someone she *could* have been.

Shai took a step forward, but when Gaotona opened the box, he revealed that the stamps weren't inside. "I'm sorry," he said. "But I think giving you these now would be a little . . . foolish on my part. It seems that any one of them could have you free from your captivity in a moment."

"Really only two of them could manage that," Shai said sourly, fingers twitching. Those soulstamps represented over eight years of her life's work. She'd started the first on the day she ended her apprenticeship.

"Hm, yes," Gaotona said. Inside the small box lay sheets of metal inscribed with the separate smaller stamps that made up the blueprints of the revisions to her soul. "This one, I believe?" He held up one of the sheets. "Shaizan. Translated . . . Shai of the Fist? This would make a warrior out of you, if you stamped yourself?"

"Yes," Shai said. So he'd been studying her Essence Marks; that was how he'd grown so good at reading her stamps.

"I understand only one tenth of what is inscribed here, if that," Gaotona said. "What I find is impressive. Truly, these must have taken years to craft."

"They are . . . precious to me," Shai said, forcing herself to sit down at her desk and not fixate on the plates. If she could escape with those, she could craft a new stamp with ease. It would still take weeks, but most of her work would not be lost. But if those plates were to be destroyed . . .

Gaotona sat down in his customary chair, nonchalantly looking through the plates. From someone else, she would have felt an implied threat. *Look what I hold in my hands; look what I could do to you.* From Gaotona, however, that was not it. He was genuinely curious.

Or was he? As ever, she could not suppress her instincts. As good as she was, someone else could be better. Just as Uncle Won had warned. Could Gaotona have been playing her for a fool all along? She felt strongly she should trust her assessment of Gaotona. But if she was wrong, it could be a disaster.

It might be anyway, she thought. *You should have run days ago.*

"Turning yourself into a soldier I understand," Gaotona said, setting aside the plate. "And this one as well. A woodsman and survivalist. That one looks extremely versatile. Impressive. And here we have a scholar. But why? You are already a scholar."

"No woman can know everything," Shai said. "There is only so much time for study. When I stamp myself with that Essence Mark, I can suddenly speak a dozen languages, from Fen to Mulla'dil—even a few from Sycla. I know dozens of different cultures and how to move in them. I know science, mathematics, and the major political factions of the world."

"Ah," Gaotona said.

Just give them to me, she thought.

"But what of this?" Gaotona said. "A beggar? Why would you want to be emaciated, and . . . is this showing that most of your hair would fall out, that your skin would become scarred?"

"It changes my appearance," Shai said. "Drastically. That's useful." She didn't mention that in that aspect, she knew the ways of the streets and survival in a city underworld. Her lock-picking skills weren't too shabby when not bearing that seal, but with it, she was incomparable.

With that stamp on her, she could probably manage to climb out the tiny window—that Mark rewrote her past to give her years of experience as a contortionist—and climb the five stories down to freedom.

"I should have realized," Gaotona said. He lifted the final plate. "That just leaves this one, most baffling of all."

Shai said nothing.

"Cooking," he said. "Farm work, sewing. Another alias, I assume. For imitating a simpler person?"

"Yes."

Gaotona nodded, putting the sheet down.

Honesty. He must see my honesty. It cannot be faked.

"No," Shai said, sighing.

He looked to her.

"It's . . . my way out," she said. "I'll never use it. It's just there, if I want to."

"Way out?"

"If I ever use that," Shai said, "it will write over my years as a Forger. Everything. I will forget how to make the simplest of stamps; I will forget that I was even apprenticed as a Forger. I will become something normal."

"And you want that?"

"No."

A pause.

"Yes. Maybe. A part of me does."

Honesty. It was so difficult. Sometimes it was the only way.

She dreamed about that simple life, on occasion. In that morbid way that someone standing at the edge of a cliff wonders what it would be like to just jump off. The temptation is there, even if it's ridiculous.

A normal life. No hiding, no lying. She loved what she did. She loved the thrill, the accomplishment, the wonder. But sometimes . . . trapped in a prison cell or running for her life . . . sometimes she dreamed of something else.

"Your aunt and uncle?" he asked. "Uncle Won, Aunt Sol, they are parts of this revision. I've read it in here."

"They're fake," Shai whispered.

"But you quote them all the time."

She squeezed her eyes shut.

"I suspect," Gaotona said, "that a life full of lying makes reality and falsehood intermix. But if you were to use this stamp, surely you would not forget everything. How would you keep the sham from yourself?"

"It would be the greatest Forgery of all," Shai said. "One intended to fool even me. Written into that is the belief that without that stamp, applied every morning, I'll die. It includes a history of illness, of visiting a . . . resealer, as you call them. A healer that works in soul-stamps. From them, my false self received a remedy, one I must apply each morning. Aunt Sol and Uncle Won would send me letters; that is part of the charade to fool myself. I've written them already. Hundreds, which— before I use the Essence Mark on myself—I will pay a delivery service good money to send periodically."

"But what if you try to visit them?" Gaotona said. "To investigate your childhood . . ."

"It's all in the plate. I will be afraid of travel. There's

truth to that, as I was indeed scared of leaving my village as a youth. Once that Mark is in place, I'll stay away from cities. I'll think the trip to visit my relatives is too dangerous. But it doesn't matter. I'll never use it."

That stamp would end her. She would forget the last twenty years, back to when she was eight and had first begun inquiring about becoming a Forger.

She'd become someone else entirely. None of the other Essence Marks did that; they rewrote some of her past, but left her with a knowledge of who she truly was. Not so with the last one. That one was to be final. It terrified her.

"This is a great deal of work for something you'll never use," Gaotona said.

"Sometimes, that is the way of life."

Gaotona shook his head.

"I was hired to destroy the painting," Shai blurted out.

She wasn't quite certain what drove her to say it. She needed to be honest with Gaotona—that was the only way her plan would work—but he didn't need this piece. Did he?

Gaotona looked up.

"ShuXen hired me to destroy Frava's painting," Shai said. "That's why I burned the masterpiece, rather than sneaking it out of the gallery."

"ShuXen? But . . . he's the original artist! Why would *he* hire you to destroy one of his works?"

"Because he hates the empire," Shai said. "He painted that piece for a woman he loved. Her children gave it to the empire as a gift. ShuXen is old now, blind, barely able to move. He did not want to go to his grave knowing that one of his works was serving to glorify the Rose Empire. He begged me to burn it."

Gaotona seemed dumbfounded. He looked at her, as if trying to pierce through to her soul. Shai didn't know why he needed to bother; this conversation had already stripped her thoroughly bare.

"A master of his caliber is hard to imitate," Shai said, "particularly without the original to work from. If you think about it, you'll realize I needed his help to create those fakes. He gave me access to his studies and concepts; he told me how he'd gone about painting it. He coached me through the brush strokes."

"Why not just have you return the original to him?" Gaotona asked.

"He's dying," Shai said. "Owning a thing is meaningless to him. That painting was done for a lover. She is gone now, so he felt the painting should be as well."

"A priceless treasure," Gaotona said. "Gone because of foolish pride."

"It was *his* work!"

"Not any longer," Gaotona said. "It belonged to everyone who saw it. You should not have agreed to this. Destroying a work of art like that is *never* right." He hesitated. "But still, I think I can understand. What you did had a nobility to it. Your goal was the Moon Scepter. Exposing yourself to destroy that painting was dangerous."

"ShuXen tutored me in painting as a youth," she said. "I could not deny his request."

Gaotona did not seem to agree, but he did seem to understand. Nights, but Shai felt exposed.

This is important to do, she told herself. *And maybe . . .*

But he did not give her the plates back. She hadn't expected him to, not now. Not until their agreement was done—an agreement she was certain she would not live to see the end of, unless she escaped.

They worked through the last group of new stamps. Each one took for at least a minute, as she'd been almost certain they would. She had the vision now, the idea of the final soul as it would be. Once she finished the sixth stamp for the day, Gaotona waited for the next.

"That's it," Shai said.

"All for today?"

"All forever," Shai said, tucking away the last of the stamps.

"You're done?" Gaotona asked, sitting up straight. "Almost a month early! It's—"

"I'm *not* done," Shai said. "Now is the most difficult part. I have to carve those several hundred stamps in tiny detail, melding them together, then create a linchpin stamp. What I've done so far is like getting all of the paints ready, creating the color and figure studies.

Now I have to put it all together. The last time I did this, it took the better part of five months."

"And you have only twenty-four days."

"And I have only twenty-four days," Shai said, but felt an immediate stab of guilt. She *had* to run. Soon. She couldn't wait to finish the project.

"Then I will leave you to it," Gaotona said, standing and rolling down his sleeve.

Day Eighty-Five

YES, SHAI THOUGHT, scrambling along the side of her bed and rifling through her stack of papers there. The table wasn't big enough. She'd pulled her sheets tight and turned the bed into a place to set all of her stacks. *Yes, his first love was from the storybook.* That was why . . . Kurshina's red hair . . . But this would be subconscious. He wouldn't know it. Embedded deeply, then.

How had she missed that? She wasn't nearly as close to being done as she'd thought. There wasn't time!

Shai added what she'd discovered to the seal she was working on, one that combined all of the various parts of Ashravan's romantic inclinations and experiences. She included it all: the embarrassing, the shameful, the glorious. Everything she'd been able to discover, and then a little bit more, calculated risks to fill out the soul. A flirtatious encounter with a woman whose name Ashravan could not recall. Idle fancies. A near affair with a woman now dead.

This was the most difficult part of the soul for Shai to imitate, for it was the most private. Little an emperor did was ever truly secret, but Ashravan had not always been emperor.

She had to extrapolate, lest she leave the soul bare, without passion.

So private, so *powerful*. She felt closest to Ashravan as she teased out these details. Not as a voyeur; by this point, she was a part of him.

She kept two books now. The formal notes of her process said she was horribly behind; that book left out details. The other book was her true one, disguised as useless piles of notes, random and haphazard.

She really was behind, but not so far as her official documentation showed. Hopefully, that subterfuge would earn her a few extra days before Frava struck.

As Shai searched for a specific note, she ran across one of her lists for escape plans. She hesitated. *First, deal with the seal on the door*, the note read in cypher. *Second, silence the guards. Third, recover your Essence Marks, if possible. Fourth, escape the palace. Fifth, escape the city.*

She'd written further notes for the execution of each step. She wasn't ignoring the escape, not completely. She had good plans.

Her frantic attempt to finish the soul, however, drew most of her attention. *One more week*, she told herself.

If I take one more week, I will finish five days before the deadline. Then I can run.

Day Ninety-Seven

"HEY," HURLI SAID, bending down. "What's this?"

Hurli was a brawny Striker who acted dumber than he was. It let him win at cards. He had two children—girls, both under the age of five—but was seeing one of the women guards on the side. Hurli secretly wished he could have been a carpenter like his father. He also would have been horrified if he'd realized how much Shai knew about him.

He held up the sheet of paper he'd found on the ground. The Bloodsealer had just left. It was the morning of the ninety-sixth day of Shai's captivity in the room, and she'd decided to put the plan into motion. She *had* to get out.

The emperor's seal was not yet finished. *Almost.* One more night's work, and she'd have it. Her plan required one more night of waiting anyway.

"Weedfingers must have dropped it," Yil said,

walking over. She was the other guard in the room this morning.

"What is it?" Shai asked from the desk.

"Letter," Hurli said with a grunt.

Both guards fell silent as they read. Palace Strikers were all literate. It was required of any imperial civil servant of at least the second reed.

Shai sat quietly, tense, sipping a cup of lemon tea and forcing herself to breathe calmly. She made herself relax even though relaxing was the last thing she wanted to do. Shai knew the letter's contents by heart. She'd written it, after all, then had dropped it covertly behind the Bloodsealer as he'd rushed out moments ago.

Brother, the letter read. *I have almost completed my task here, and the wealth I have earned will rival even that of Azalec after his work in the Southern Provinces. The captive I secure is hardly worth the effort, but who am I to question the reasoning of people paying me far too much money?*

I will return to you shortly. I am proud to say that my other mission here has been a success. I have identified several capable warriors, and have gathered sufficient samples from them. Hair, fingernails, and a few personal effects that will not be missed. I feel confident that we will have our personal guards very soon.

It went on, the writing covering both the front and the back, so that it didn't look suspicious. Shai had padded it with a lot of talk about the palace, including things that others would assume that Shai didn't know but that the Bloodsealer would.

Shai worried that the letter was too overt. Would the guards find it to be an obvious forgery?

"That KuNuKam," Yil whispered, using a native word of theirs. It roughly translated as a man who had an anus for a mouth. "That imperial KuNuKam!"

Apparently, they believed it really was from him. Subtlety could be lost on soldiers.

"Can I see it?" Shai asked.

Hurli held it out to her. "Is he saying what I think?" the guard asked. "He's been . . . *gathering* things from us?"

"It might not mean the Strikers," Shai said after reading the letter. "He doesn't say."

"Why would he want hair?" Yil asked. "And fingernails?"

"They can do things with pieces of you," Hurli said, then cursed again. "You see what he does each day on the door with Shai's blood."

"I don't know if he could do much with hair or fingernails," Shai said skeptically. "This is just bravado. Blood needs to be fresh, not more than a day old, for it to work in his stamps. He's bragging to his brother."

"He shouldn't be doing things like that," Hurli said.

"I wouldn't worry about it," Shai said.

The other two shared looks. In a few minutes, the guard change occurred. Hurli and Yil left, muttering to one another, the letter shoved in Hurli's pocket. They weren't likely to hurt the Bloodsealer badly. Threaten him, yes.

The Bloodsealer was known to frequent teahouses in the area each evening. Almost she felt sorry for the man. She had deduced that when he got news from home, he was quick and punctual to her door. He sometimes looked excited. When he didn't get news, he drank. This morning, he had looked sad. No news in a while, then.

What happened to him tonight would not make his day any better. Yes, Shai almost felt sorry for him, but then she remembered the seal on the door and the bandage she'd tied on her arm after he'd drawn blood today.

As soon as the guard change was accomplished, Shai took a deep breath, then dug back into her work.

Tonight. Tonight, she would finish.

Day Ninety-Eight

SHAI KNELT ON THE FLOOR amid a pattern of scattered pages, each filled with cramped script or drawings of seals. Behind her, morning opened her eyes, and sunlight seeped through the stained glass window, spraying the room with crimson, blue, violet.

A single soulstamp, carved from polished stone, rested facedown on a metal plate sitting before her. Soulstone, as a rock, looked not unlike soapstone or another fine-grained stone, but with bits of red mixed in. As if drops of blood had stained it.

Shai blinked tired eyes. Was she really going to try to escape? She'd had . . . what? Four hours of sleep in the last three days combined?

Surely escape could wait. Surely she could rest, just for today.

Rest, she thought numbly, *and I will not wake.*

She remained in place, kneeling. That stamp seemed the most beautiful thing she had ever seen.

Her ancestors had worshipped rocks that fell from the sky at night. The souls of broken gods, those chunks had been called. Master craftsmen would carve them to bring out the shape. Once, Shai had found that foolish. Why worship something you yourself created?

Kneeling before her masterpiece, she understood. She felt as if she'd bled everything into that stamp. She had pressed two years' worth of effort into three months, then had topped it off with a night of desperate, frantic carving. During that night, she'd made changes to her notes, to the soul itself. Drastic changes. She still didn't know if they had been provoked by her final, awesome vision of the project as a whole . . . or if those changes had instead been faulty ideas born of fatigue and delusion.

She wouldn't know until the stamp was used.

"Is it . . . is it done?" asked one of her guards. The two of them had moved to the far edge of the room, to sit beside the hearth and give her room on the floor. She vaguely remembered shoving aside the furniture. She'd spent part of the time pulling stacks of paper out from their place beneath the bed, then crawling under to fetch others.

Was it done?

Shai nodded.

"What is it?" the guard asked.

Nights, she thought. *That's right. They don't even know.* The common guards left each day during her conversations with Gaotona.

The poor Strikers would probably find themselves assigned to some remote outpost of the empire for the rest of their lives, guarding the passes leading down to the distant Teoish Peninsula or the like. They would be quietly brushed under the rug to keep them from revealing, even accidentally, anything of what had happened here.

"Ask Gaotona if you want to know," Shai said softly. "I am not allowed to say."

Shai reverently picked up the seal, then placed both it and its plate inside a box she had prepared. The stamp nestled in red velvet, the plate—shaped like a large, thin medallion—in an indentation underneath the lid. She closed the lid, then pulled over a second, slightly larger box. Inside lay five seals, carved and prepared for her upcoming escape. If she managed it. Two of them she'd already used.

If she could just sleep for a few hours. Just a few . . .

No. I can't use the bed anyway.

Curling up on the floor sounded wonderful, however.

The door began to open. Shai felt a sudden, striking moment of panic. Was it the Bloodsealer? He was supposed to be stuck in bed, having drunk himself to a stupor after being roughed up by the Strikers!

For a moment, she felt a strange guilty sense of relief.

If the Bloodsealer had come, she wouldn't have a chance to escape today. She could sleep. Had Hurli and Yil not thrashed him? Shai had been sure that she'd read them correctly, and . . .

. . . and, in her fatigue, she realized she'd been jumping to conclusions. The door opened all the way, and someone did enter, but it was not the Bloodsealer.

It was Captain Zu.

"Out," he barked at the two guards.

They jumped into motion.

"In fact," Zu said, "you're relieved for the day. I'll watch until the shift changes."

The two saluted and left. Shai felt like a wounded elk being abandoned by the herd. The door clicked closed, and Zu slowly, deliberately, turned to look at her.

"The stamp isn't ready yet," Shai lied. "So you can—"

"It doesn't need to be ready," Zu said, smiling a wide, thick-lipped smile. "I believe I promised you something three months ago, thief. We have an . . . unsettled debt."

The room was dim, her lamp having burned low and morning only just breaking. Shai backed away from him, quickly revising her plans. This *wasn't* how it was supposed to go. She couldn't fight Zu.

Her mouth kept moving, keeping him distracted but also playing a part she devised for herself on the fly. "When Frava finds out you came here," Shai said, "she will be furious."

Zu drew his sword.

"Nights!" Shai said, backing up to her bed. "Zu, you don't need to do this. You *can't* do this. I have work that needs to be done!"

"Another will complete your work," Zu said, leering. "Frava has another Forger. You think you're so clever. You probably have some wonderful escape planned for tomorrow. This time, we're striking first. You didn't anticipate *this,* did you, liar? I'm going to enjoy killing you. Enjoy it so much."

He lunged with the sword, its tip catching her blouse and ripping a line through it at her side. Shai jumped away, shouting for help. She was still playing the part, but it did not require acting. Her heart thumped, panic rising, as she rounded the bed in a scramble, putting it between herself and Zu.

He smiled broadly, then jumped for her, leaping onto the bed.

It promptly collapsed. During the night, while crawling under the bed to get her notes, she had Forged the wood of the frame to have deep flaws, attacked by insects, making it fragile. She'd cut the mattress underneath in wide slashes.

Zu barely had time to shout as the bed broke completely away, crashing into the pit she'd opened in the floor below. The water damage to her room— the mildew she'd smelled when first entering—had been key. By reports, the wooden beams above would have rotted and the ceiling would have fallen in if they hadn't located the leak as quickly as they had. A simple Forgery, very plausible, made it so that the floor *had* fallen in.

Zu crashed into the empty storage room one story down. Shai stood puffing, then peered into the hole. The man lay among the broken remnants of the bed. Some of that had been stuffing and cushioning. He would probably live—she'd been intending this trap for one of the regular guards, of whom she was fond.

Not exactly how I planned it, she thought, *but workable.*

Shai rushed to the table and gathered her things. The box of stamps, the emperor's soul, some extra soulstone and ink. And the two books explaining the stamps she had created in deep complexity—the official one, and the true one.

She tossed the official one into the hearth as she passed. Then she stopped in front of the door, counting heartbeats.

She agonized, watching the Bloodsealer's mark as it pulsed. Finally, after a few tormenting minutes, the seal on the door flashed one last time . . . then faded. The Bloodsealer had not returned in time to renew it.

Freedom.

Shai burst out into the hallway, abandoning her home of the last three months, a room now trimmed in gold and silver. The hallway outside had been so near, yet it felt like another country entirely. She pressed the third of her prepared stamps against her buttoned blouse, changing it to match that of the palace servants, with official insignia embroidered on the left breast.

She had little time to make her next move. Soon, either the Bloodsealer would make his way to her room, Zu would wake from his fall, or the guards would arrive for the shift change. Shai wanted to run down the hallway, breaking for the palace stables.

She did not. Running implied one of two things—guilt or an important task. Either would be memorable. Instead, she kept her gait to a swift walk and adopted the expression of one who knew what she was doing, and so should not be interrupted.

She soon entered the better-used sections of the enormous palace. No one stopped her. At a certain carpeted intersection, she stopped herself.

To the right, down a long hallway, lay the entrance to the emperor's chambers. The seal she carried in her right hand, boxed and cushioned, seemed to leap in her fingers. Why hadn't she left it in the room for Gaotona to discover? The arbiters would hunt her less assiduously if they had the seal.

She could just leave it here, in this hallway lined with portraits of ancient rulers and cluttered with Forged urns from ancient eras.

No. She had brought it with her for a reason. She'd prepared tools to get into the emperor's chambers. She'd known all along this was what she would do.

If she left now, she'd never *truly* know if the seal

worked. That would be like building a house, then never stepping inside. Like forging a sword, and never giving it a swing. Like crafting a masterpiece of art, then locking it away to never be seen again.

Shai started down the long hallway.

As soon as no one was directly in sight, she turned over one of those horrid urns and broke the seal on the bottom. It transformed back into a blank clay version of itself.

She'd had plenty of time to find out exactly where these urns were crafted and by whom. The fourth of her prepared stamps transformed the urn into a replica of an ornate golden chamber pot. Shai strode down the hallway to the emperor's quarters, then nodded to the guards, chamber pot under her arm.

"I don't recognize you," one guard said. She didn't recognize him either, with that scarred face and squinty look. As she'd expected. The guards set to watching her had been kept separate from the others so they couldn't talk about their duties.

"Oh," Shai said, fumbling, looking abashed. "I am sorry, greater one. I was only assigned this task this morning." She blushed, fishing out of her pocket a small square of thick paper, marked with Gaotona's seal and signature. She had forged both the old-fashioned way. Very convenient, how he'd let her tell him how to maintain security on the emperor's rooms.

She got through without any further difficulty. The

next three rooms of the emperor's expansive chambers were empty. Beyond them was a locked door. She had to Forge the wood of that door into some that had been damaged by insects—using the same stamp she'd used on her bed—to get through. It didn't take for long, but a few seconds was enough for her to kick the door open.

Inside, she found the emperor's bedroom. It was the same place she'd been led on that first day when she'd been offered this chance. The room was empty save for him, lying in that bed. He was awake, but stared sightlessly at the ceiling.

The room was still. Quiet. It smelled . . . too clean. Too white. Like a blank canvas.

Shai walked up to the side of the bed. Ashravan didn't look at her. His eyes didn't move. She rested fingers on his shoulder. He had a handsome face, though he was some fifteen years her senior. That was not much for a Grand; they lived longer than most.

His was a strong face, despite his long time abed. Golden hair, a firm chin, a nose that was prominent. So different in features from Shai's people.

"I know your soul," Shai said softly. "I know it better than you ever did."

No alarm yet. Shai continued to expect one any moment, but she knelt down beside the bed anyway. "I wish that I could know you. Not your soul, but *you*. I've read about you; I've seen into your heart.

I've rebuilt your soul, as best I could. But that isn't the same. It isn't knowing someone, is it? That's knowing *about* someone."

Was that a cry outside, from a distant part of the palace?

"I don't ask much of you," she said softly. "Just that you live. Just that you *be*. I've done what I can. Let it be enough."

She took a deep breath, then opened the box and took out his Essence Mark. She inked it, then pulled up his shirt, exposing the upper arm.

Shai hesitated, then pressed the stamp down. It hit flesh, and stayed frozen for a moment, as stamps always did. The skin and muscle didn't give way until a second later, when the stamp *sank* a fraction of an inch.

She twisted the stamp, locking it in, and pulled it back. The bright red seal glowed faintly.

Ashravan blinked.

Shai rose and stepped back as he sat up and looked around. Silently, she counted.

"My rooms," Ashravan said. "What happened? There was an attack. I was . . . I was wounded. Oh, mother of lights. Kurshina. She's dead."

His face became a mask of grief, but he covered it a second later. He was emperor. He might have a temper, but so long as he was not enraged, he was good at covering what he felt. He turned to her, and living eyes—eyes that *saw*—focused on her. "Who are you?"

The question twisted her insides, for all the fact that she'd expected it.

"I'm a kind of surgeon," Shai said. "You were wounded badly. I have healed you. However, what I used to do so is considered . . . unsavory by some parts of your culture."

"You're a resealer," he said. "A . . . a Forger?"

"In a way," Shai said. He would believe that because he wanted to. "This was a difficult type of resealing. You will have to be stamped each day, and you must keep that metal plate—the one shaped like a disc in that box—with you at all times. Without these, you die, Ashravan."

"Give it to me," he said, holding his hand out for the stamp.

She hesitated. She wasn't certain why.

"Give it to me," he said, more forceful.

She placed the stamp in his hand.

"Don't tell anyone what has happened here," she said to him. "Neither guards nor servants. Only your arbiters know of what I have done."

The cries outside sounded louder. Ashravan looked toward them. "If no one is to know," he said, "you must go. Leave this place and do not return." He looked down at the seal. "I should probably have you killed for knowing my secret."

That was the selfishness he'd learned during his years in the palace. Yes, she'd gotten that right.

"But you won't," she said.

"I won't."

141

And there was the mercy, buried deeply.

"Go before I change my mind," he said.

She took one step toward the doorway, then checked her pocket watch—well over a minute. The stamp had taken, at least for the short term. She turned and looked at him.

"What are you waiting for?" he demanded.

"I just wanted one more glimpse," she said.

He frowned.

The shouts grew even louder.

"Go," he said. "Please." He seemed to know what those shouts were about, or at least he could guess.

"Do better this time," Shai said. "Please."

With that, she fled.

She had been tempted, for a time, to write into him a desire to protect her. There would have been no good reason for it, at least in his eyes, and it might have undermined the entire Forgery. Beyond that, she didn't believe that he *could* save her. Until his period of mourning was through, he could not leave his quarters or speak to anyone other than his arbiters. During that time, the arbiters ran the empire.

They practically ran it anyway. No, a hasty revision of Ashravan's soul to protect her would not have worked. Near the last door out, Shai picked up her fake chamber pot. She hefted it, then stumbled through the doors. She gasped audibly at the distant cries.

"Is that about *me?*" Shai cried. "Nights! I didn't mean

it! I know I wasn't supposed to see him. I know he's in seclusion, but I opened the wrong door!"

The guards stared at her, then one relaxed. "It isn't you. Find your quarters and stay there."

Shai bobbed a bow and hastened away. Most of the guards didn't know her, and so—

She felt a sharp pain at her side. She gasped. That pain felt like it did each morning, when the Bloodsealer stamped the door.

Panicked, Shai felt at her side. The cut in her blouse— where Zu had slashed her with his sword—had gone all the way through her dark undershirt! When her fingers came back, they had a couple of drops of blood on them. Just a nick, nothing dangerous. In the scramble, she hadn't even noticed she'd been cut.

But the tip of Zu's sword . . . it had her blood on it. Fresh blood. The Bloodsealer had found that and had begun the hunt. That pain meant he was locating her, was attuning his pets to her.

Shai tossed the urn aside and started running.

Staying hidden was no longer a consideration. Remaining unremarkable was pointless. If the Bloodsealer's skeletals reached her, she'd die. That was it. She had to reach a horse soon, then stay ahead of the skeletals for twenty-four hours, until her blood grew stale.

Shai dashed through the hallways. Servants began pointing, others screamed. She almost bowled over a southern ambassador in red priest's armor.

Shai cursed, bolting around the man. The palace exits would be locked down by now. She *knew* that. She'd studied the security. Getting out would be nearly impossible.

Always have a backup, Uncle Won said.

She always did.

Shai stopped in the hallway, and determined—as she should have earlier—that running for the exits was pointless. She was in a near panic, with the Bloodsealer on her trail, but she *had* to think clearly.

Backup plan. Hers was a desperate one, but it was all she had. She started running again, skidding around a corner, doubling back the way she'd just come.

Nights, let me have guessed right about him, she thought. *If he's secretly a master charlatan beyond my skill, I am doomed. Oh, Unknown God, please. This time, let me be right.*

Heart racing, fatigue forgotten in the moment, she eventually skidded to a stop in the hallway leading to the emperor's rooms.

There she waited. The guards inspected her, frowning, but held their posts at the end of the hallway as they'd been trained. They called to her. It was hard to keep from moving. That Bloodsealer was getting closer and closer with his horrible pets . . .

"Why are you here?" a voice said.

Shai turned as Gaotona stepped into the hallway. He'd come for the emperor first. The others would search for Shai, but Gaotona would come for the emperor, to be certain he was safe.

Shai stepped up to him, anxious. *This,* she thought, *is probably my worst idea ever for a backup plan.*

"It worked," she said softly.

"You tried the stamp?" Gaotona said, taking her arm and glancing at the guards, then pulling her aside well out of earshot. "Of all the hasty, insane, foolish—"

"It *worked,* Gaotona," Shai said.

"Why did you come to him? Why not run while you had the chance?"

"I had to know. I *had* to."

He looked at her, meeting her eyes. Seeing through them, into her soul, as he always did. Nights, but he would have made a wonderful Forger.

"The Bloodsealer has your trail," Gaotona said. "He has summoned those . . . *things* to catch you."

"I know."

Gaotona hesitated for only a moment, then brought out a wooden box from his voluminous pockets. Shai's heart leaped.

He handed it toward her, and she took it with one hand, but he did not let go. "You knew I'd come here," Gaotona said. "You knew I'd have these, and that I'd give them to you. I've been played for a fool."

Shai said nothing.

"How did you do it?" he asked. "I thought I watched you carefully. I was *certain* I had not been manipulated.

And yet I ran here, half knowing I'd find you. Knowing you'd need these. I *still* didn't realize until this very moment that you'd probably planned all of this."

"I did manipulate you, Gaotona," she admitted. "But I had to do it in the most difficult way possible."

"Which was?"

"By being genuine," she replied.

"You can't manipulate people by being genuine."

"You can't?" Shai asked. "Is that not how you've made your entire career? Speaking honestly, teaching people what to expect of you, then expecting them to be honest to you in return?"

"It's not the same thing."

"No," she said. "It's not. But it was the best I could manage. Everything I've said to you is true, Gaotona. The painting I destroyed, the secrets about my life and desires . . . Being genuine. It was the only way to get you on my side."

"I'm not on your side." He paused. "But I don't want you killed either, girl. Particularly not by those *things*. Take these. Days! Take them and go, before I change my mind."

"Thank you," she whispered, pulling the box to her breast. She fished in her skirt pocket and brought out a small, thick book. "Keep this safe," she said. "Show it to no one."

He took it hesitantly. "What is it?"

"The truth," she said, then leaned in and kissed him

on the cheek. "If I escape, I will change my final Essence Mark. The one I never intend to use . . . I will add to it, and to my memories, a kindly grandfather who saved my life. A man of wisdom and compassion whom I respected very much."

"Go, fool girl," he said. He actually had a tear in his eye. If she hadn't been on the very edge of panic, she'd have felt proud of that. And ashamed of her pride. That was how she was.

"Ashravan lives," she said. "When you think of me, remember that. It *worked*. Nights, it *worked!*"

She left him, dashing down the corridor.

Gaotona listened to the girl go, but did not turn to watch her flee. He stared at that door to the emperor's chambers. Two confused guards, and a passage into . . . what?

The future of the Rose Empire.

We will be led by someone not truly alive, Gaotona thought. *The fruits of our foul labors.*

He took a deep breath, then walked past the guards and pushed open the doors to go and look upon the thing he had wrought.

Just . . . please, let it not be a monster.

Shai strode down the palace hallway, holding the box of seals. She ripped off her buttoned blouse—revealing the tight, black cotton shirt she wore underneath—and tucked it into her pocket. She left on her skirt and the leggings beneath. It wasn't so different from the clothing she'd trained in.

Servants scattered around her. They knew, just from her posture, to get out of the way. Suddenly, Shai felt more confident than she had in years.

She had her soul back. All of it.

She took out one of her Essence Marks as she walked. She inked it with bold strikes and returned the box of seals to her skirt pocket. Then, she slammed the seal against her right bicep and locked it into place, rewriting her history, her memories, her life experience.

In that fraction of a moment, she remembered both histories. She remembered two years spent locked away, planning, creating the Essence Mark. She remembered a lifetime of being a Forger.

At the same time, she remembered spending the last fifteen years among the Teullu people. They had adopted her and trained her in their martial arts.

Two places at once, two timelines at once.

Then the former faded, and she became Shaizan, the name the Teullu had given her. Her body became leaner, harder. The body of a warrior. She slipped off her spectacles. Her eyes had been healed long ago, and she didn't need those any longer.

Gaining access to the Teullu training had been difficult; they did not like outsiders. She'd nearly been killed by them a dozen different times during her year training. But she had succeeded.

She lost all knowledge of how to create stamps, all sense of scholarly inclination. She was still herself, and she remembered her immediate past—being captured, forced to sit in that cell. She retained knowledge—logically—of what she'd just done with the stamp to her arm, and knew that the life she now remembered was fake.

But she didn't *feel* that it was. As that seal burned on her arm, she became the version of herself that would have existed if she'd been adopted by a harsh warrior culture and lived among them for well over a decade.

She kicked off her shoes. Her hair shortened; a scar stretched from her nose down around her right cheek. She walked like a warrior, prowling instead of striding.

She reached the servants' section of the palace just before the stables, the Imperial Gallery to her left.

A door opened in front of her. Zu, tall and wide-lipped, pushed through. He had a gash on his forehead—blood seeped through the bandage there—and his clothing had been torn by his fall.

He had a tempest in his eyes. He sneered as he saw her. "You've done it now. The Bloodsealer led us right to you. I'm going to enjoy—"

He cut off as Shaizan stepped forward in a blur and smacked the heel of her hand against his wrist, breaking it, knocking the sword from his fingers. She snapped her hand upward, chopping him in the throat. Then she curled her fingers into a fist and placed a tight, short, full-knuckled punch into his chest. Six ribs shattered.

Zu stumbled backward, gasping, eyes wide with absolute shock. His sword clanged to the ground. Shaizan stepped past him, pulling his knife from his belt and whipping it up to cut the tie on his cloak.

Zu toppled to the floor, leaving the cloak in her fingers.

Shai might have said something to him. Shaizan didn't have the patience for witticisms or gibes. A warrior kept moving, like a river. She didn't break stride as she whipped the cloak around and entered the hallway behind Zu.

He gasped for breath. He'd live, but he wouldn't hold a sword again for months.

Movement came from the end of the hallway: white-limbed creatures, too thin to be alive. Shaizan prepared herself with a wide stance, body turned to the side, facing down the hallway, knees slightly bent. It did not matter how many monstrosities the Bloodsealer had; it did not matter if she won or lost.

The challenge mattered. That was all.

There were five, in the shape of men with swords. They scrambled down the hall, bones clattering, eyeless skulls regarding her without expression beyond that of their ever-grinning, pointed teeth. Some bits of the skeletals had been replaced by wooden carvings to fix bones that had broken in battle. Each creature bore a glowing red seal on its forehead; blood was required to give them life.

Even Shaizan had never fought monsters like this before. Stabbing them would be useless. But those bits that had been replaced . . . some were pieces of rib or other bones the skeletals shouldn't need to fight. So if bones were broken or removed, would the creature stop working?

It seemed her best chance. She did not consider further. Shaizan was a creature of instinct. As the things reached her, she whipped Zu's cloak around and tossed it over the head of the first one. It thrashed, striking at the cloak as she engaged the second creature.

She caught its attack on the blade of Zu's dagger, then stepped up so close she could smell its bones, and reached in just below the thing's rib cage. She grabbed the spine and yanked, pulling free a handful of vertebrae, the tip of the sternum cutting her forearm. All of the bones of each skeletal seemed to be sharpened.

It collapsed, bones clattering. She was right. With

the pivotal bones removed, the thing could no longer animate. Shaizan tossed the handful of vertebrae aside.

That left four of them. From what little she knew, skeletals did not tire and were relentless. She had to be quick, or they would overwhelm her.

The three behind attacked her; Shaizan ducked away, getting around the first one as it pulled off the cloak. She grabbed its skull by the eye sockets, earning a deep cut in the arm from its sword as she did so. Her blood sprayed against the wall as she yanked the skull free; the rest of the creature's body dropped to the ground in a heap.

Keep moving. Don't slow.

If she slowed, she died.

She spun on the other three, using the skull to block one sword strike and the dagger to deflect another. She skirted around the third, and it scored her side.

She could not feel pain. She'd trained herself to ignore it in battle. That was good, because that one would have *hurt*.

She smashed the skull into the head of another skeletal, shattering both. It dropped, and Shaizan spun between the other two. Their backhand strikes clanged against one another. Shaizan's kick sent one of them stumbling back, and she rammed her body against the other, crushing it up against the wall. The bones pushed together, and she got hold of the spine, then yanked free some of the vertebrae.

The creature's bones fell with a racket. Shaizan wavered as she righted herself. Too much blood lost. She was slowing. When had she dropped the dagger? It must have slipped from her fingers as she slammed the creature against the wall.

Focus. One left.

It charged her, a sword in each hand. She heaved herself forward—getting inside its reach before it could swing—and grabbed its forearm bones. She couldn't pull them free, not from that angle. She grunted, keeping the swords at bay. Barely. She was weakening.

It pressed closer. Shaizan growled, blood flowing freely from her arm and side.

She head-butted the thing.

That worked worse in real life than it did in stories. Shaizan's vision dimmed and she slipped to her knees, gasping. The skeletal fell before her, cracked skull rolling free from the force of the blow. Blood dripped down the side of her face. She'd split her forehead, perhaps cracked her own skull.

She fell to her side and fought for consciousness.

Slowly, the darkness retreated.

Shaizan found herself amid scattered bones in an otherwise empty hallway of stone. The only color was that of her blood.

She had won. Another challenge met. She howled a chant of her adopted family, then retrieved her dagger and cut off pieces of her blouse. She used them to bind her wounds. The blood loss was bad. Even a woman with her training would not be meeting any further challenges today. Not if they required strength.

She managed to rise and retrieve Zu's cloak—still immobilized by pain, he watched her with amazed eyes. She gathered all five skulls of the Bloodsealer's pets and tied them in the cloak.

That done, she continued down the hallway, trying to project strength—not the fatigue, dizziness, and pain she actually felt.

He will be here somewhere . . .

She yanked open a storage closet at the end of the hall and found the Bloodsealer on the floor inside, eyes glazed by the shock of having his pets destroyed in rapid succession.

Shaizan grabbed the front of his shirt and hauled him to his feet. The move almost made her pass out again. *Careful.*

The Bloodsealer whimpered.

"Go back to your swamp," Shaizan growled softly. "The one waiting for you doesn't care that you're in the capital, that you're making so much money, that you're doing it all for her. She wants you home. That's why her letters are worded as they are."

Shaizan said that part for Shai, who would feel guilty if she did not.

The man looked at her, confused. "How do you . . . *Ahhrgh!*"

He said the last part as Shaizan rammed her dagger into his leg. He collapsed as she released his shirt.

"That," Shaizan said to him softly, leaning down, "is so that I have some of your blood. Do not hunt me. You saw what I did to your pets. I will do worse to you. I'm taking the skulls, so you cannot send them for me again. *Go. Back. Home.*"

He nodded weakly. She left him in a heap, cowering and holding his bleeding leg. The arrival of the skeletals had driven everyone else away, including guards. Shaizan stalked toward the stables, then stopped, thinking of something. It wasn't too far off . . .

You're nearly dead from these wounds, she told herself. *Don't be a fool.*

She decided to be a fool anyway.

A short time later, Shaizan entered the stables and found only a couple of frightened stable hands there. She chose the most distinctive mount in the stables. So it was that—wearing Zu's cloak and hunkered down on his horse—Shaizan was able to gallop out of the palace gates, and not a man or woman tried to stop her.

"Was she telling the truth, Gaotona?" Ashravan asked, regarding himself in the mirror.

Gaotona looked up from where he sat. *Was she?* he thought to himself. He could never tell with Shai.

Ashravan had insisted upon dressing himself, though he was obviously weak from his long stay in bed. Gaotona sat on a stool nearby, trying to sort through a deluge of emotions.

"Gaotona?" Ashravan asked, turning to him. "I was wounded, as that woman said? You went to a *Forger* to heal me, rather than our trained resealers?"

"Yes, Your Majesty."

The expressions, Gaotona thought. *How did she get those right? The way he frowns just before asking a question? The way he cocks his head when not answered immediately. The way he stands, the way he waves his fingers when he's saying something he thinks is particularly important . . .*

"A MaiPon Forger," the emperor said, pulling on his golden coat. "I hardly think *that* was necessary."

"Your wounds were beyond the skill of our resealers."

"I thought nothing was beyond them."

"We did as well."

The emperor regarded the red seal on his arm. His expression tightened. "This will be a manacle, Gaotona. A weight."

"You will suffer it."

Ashravan turned toward him. "I see that the near death of your liege has not made you any more respectful, old man."

"I have been tired lately, Your Majesty."

"You're judging me," Ashravan said, looking back at the mirror. "You always do. Days alight! One day I will rid myself of you. You realize that, don't you? It's only because of past service that I even consider keeping you around."

It was uncanny. This *was* Ashravan; a Forgery so keen, so perfect, that Gaotona would never have guessed the truth if he hadn't already known. He wanted to believe that the emperor's soul had still been there, in his body, and that the seal had simply . . . uncovered it.

That would be a convenient lie to tell himself. Perhaps Gaotona would start believing it eventually. Unfortunately, he had seen the emperor's eyes before, and he knew . . . he *knew* what Shai had done.

"I will go to the other arbiters, Your Majesty," Gaotona said, standing. "They will wish to see you."

"Very well. You are dismissed."

Gaotona walked toward the door.

"Gaotona."

He turned.

"Three months in bed," the emperor said, regarding himself in the mirror, "with no one allowed to see me. The resealers couldn't do anything. They can fix any normal wound. It was something to do with my mind, wasn't it?"

He wasn't supposed to figure that out, Gaotona thought. *She said she wasn't going to write it into him.*

But Ashravan had been a clever man. Beneath it all, he had *always* been clever. Shai had restored him, and she couldn't keep him from thinking.

"Yes, Your Majesty," Gaotona said.

Ashravan grunted. "You are fortunate your gambit worked. You could have ruined my ability to think— you could have sold my soul itself. I'm not sure if I should punish you or reward you for taking that risk."

"I assure you, Your Majesty," Gaotona said as he left, "I have given myself both great rewards and great punishments during these last few months."

He left then, letting the emperor stare at himself in the mirror and consider the implications of what had been done.

For better or worse, they had their emperor back.

Or, at least, a copy of him.

Epilogue:
Day One Hundred and One

"AND SO I HOPE," Ashravan said to the assembled arbiters of the eighty factions, "that I have laid to rest certain pernicious rumors. Exaggerations of my illness were, obviously, wishful fancy. We have yet to discover who sent the assassins, but the murder of the empress is *not* something that will go ignored." He looked over the arbiters. "Nor will it go unanswered."

Frava folded her arms, watching the copy with satisfaction, but also displeasure. *What back doors did you put into his mind, little thief?* Frava wondered. *We will find them.*

Nyen was already inspecting copies of the seals. The Forger claimed that he could retroactively decrypt them, though it would take time. Perhaps years. Still, Frava would eventually know how to control the emperor.

Destroying the notes had been clever on the girl's part. Had she guessed, somehow, that Frava wasn't really making copies? Frava shook her head and stepped up beside Gaotona, who sat in their box of the Theater of Address. She sat down beside him, speaking very softly. "They are accepting it."

Gaotona nodded, his eyes on the fake emperor. "There isn't even a whisper of suspicion. What we did . . . it was not only audacious, it would be presumed impossible."

"The girl could put a knife to our throats," Frava said. "The proof of what we did is burned into the emperor's own body. We will need to tread carefully in coming years."

Gaotona nodded, looking distracted. Days afire, how Frava wished she could get him removed from his station. He was the only one of the arbiters who ever took a stand against her. Just before his assassination, Ashravan had been ready to do it at her prompting.

Those meetings had been private. Shai wouldn't have known of them, so the fake would not either. Frava would have to begin the process again, unless she found a way to control this duplicate Ashravan. Both options frustrated her.

"A part of me can't believe that we actually did it," Gaotona said softly as the fake emperor moved on to the next section of his speech, a call for unity.

Frava sniffed. "The plan was sound all along."

"Shai escaped."

"She will be found."

"I doubt it," he said. "We were lucky to catch her that once. Fortunately, I do not believe we have much to worry about from her."

"She'll try to blackmail us," Frava said. *Or she'll try to find a way to control the throne.*

"No," Gaotona said. "No, she is satisfied."

"Satisfied with escaping alive?"

"Satisfied with having placed one of her creations on the throne. Once, she dared to try to fool thousands— but now she has a chance to fool millions. An entire empire. Exposing what she has done would ruin the majesty of it, in her eyes."

Did the old fool really believe that? His naiveness often presented Frava with opportunities; she'd considered letting him keep his station simply for that reason.

The fake emperor continued his speech. Ashravan *had* liked to hear himself speak. The Forger had gotten that right.

"He's using the assassination as a means of bolstering our faction," Gaotona said. "You hear? The implications that we need to unify, pull together, remember our heritage of strength . . . And the rumors, the ones the Glory Faction spread regarding him being killed . . . by mentioning them, he weakens their faction. They gambled on him not returning, and now that he has, they seem foolish."

"True," Frava said. "Did you put him up to that?"

"No," Gaotona said. "He refused to let me counsel him on his speech. This move, though, it feels like something the old Ashravan would have done, the Ashravan from a decade ago."

"The copy isn't perfect, then," Frava said. "We'll have to remember that."

"Yes," Gaotona said. He held something, a small, thick book that Frava didn't recognize.

A rustling came from the back of the box, and a servant of Frava's Symbol entered, passing Arbiters Stivient and Ushnaka. The youthful messenger came to Frava's side, then leaned down.

Frava gave the girl a displeased glance. "What can be so important that you interrupt me here?"

"I'm sorry, your grace," the woman whispered. "But you asked me to arrange your palace offices for your afternoon meetings."

"Well?" Frava asked.

"Did you enter the rooms yesterday, my lady?"

"No. With the business of that rogue Bloodsealer, and the emperor's demands, and . . ." Frava's frown deepened. "What is it?"

Shai turned and looked back at the Imperial Seat. The city rolled across a group of seven large hills; a major faction house topped each of the outer six, with the palace dominating the central hill.

The horse at her side looked little like the one she'd taken from the palace. It was missing teeth and walked with its head hanging low, back bowed. Its coat looked as if it hadn't been brushed in ages, and the creature was so underfed, its ribs poked out like the slats on the back of a chair.

Shai had spent the previous days lying low, using her beggar Essence Mark to hide in the Imperial Seat's underground. With that disguise in place, and with one on the horse, she'd escaped the city with ease. She'd removed her Mark once out, however. Thinking like the beggar was . . . uncomfortable.

Shai loosened the horse's saddle, then reached under it and placed a fingernail against the glowing seal there. She snapped the seal's rim with some effort, breaking the Forgery. The horse transformed immediately, back straightening, head rising, sides swelling. It danced uncertainly, head darting back and forth, tugging against the reins. Zu's warhorse was a fine animal, worth more than a small house in some parts of the empire.

Hidden among the supplies on his back was the painting that Shai had stolen, again, from Arbiter Frava's office. A forgery. Shai had never had cause to steal one of her own works before. It felt . . . amusing. She'd left the large frame cut open with a single Reo rune carved in the center on the wall behind. It did not have a very pleasant meaning.

She patted the horse on the neck. All things considered, this wasn't a bad haul. A fine horse and a painting that, though fake, was so realistic that even its owner had thought it was the original.

He's giving his speech right now, Shai thought. *I would like to have heard that.*

Her gem, her crowning work, wore the mantle of imperial power. That thrilled her, but the thrill had driven her onward. Even making him live again had not been the cause of her frantic work. No, in the end, she'd pushed herself so hard because she'd wanted to leave a few specific changes embedded within the soul. Perhaps those months of being genuine to Gaotona had changed her.

Copy an image over and over on a stack of paper, Shai thought, *and eventually the lower sheets will bear the same image, pressed down. Deep within.*

She turned, taking out the Essence Mark that would transform her into a survivalist and hunter. Frava would anticipate Shai using the roads, so she would instead make her way into the deep center of the nearby Sogdian Forest. Those depths would hide her well. In a few months, she would carefully proceed out of the province and continue on to her next task: tracking down the Imperial Fool, who had betrayed her.

For now, she wanted to be far away from walls,

palaces, and courtly lies. Shai hoisted herself into the horse's saddle and bid farewell to both the Imperial Seat and the man who now ruled it.

Live well, Ashravan, she thought. *And make me proud.*

Late that night, following the emperor's speech, Gaotona sat by the familiar hearth in his personal study looking at the book that Shai had given him.

And marveling.

The book was a copy of the emperor's soulstamp, in detail, with notes. Everything that Shai had done lay bare to him here.

Frava would not find an exploit to control the emperor, because there wasn't one. The emperor's soul was complete, locked tight, and all his own. That wasn't to say that he was exactly the same as he had been.

I took some liberties, as you can see, Shai's notes explained. *I wanted to replicate his soul as precisely as possible. That was the task and the challenge. I did so.*

Then I took the soul a few steps farther, strengthening some memories, weakening others. I embedded deep within Ashravan triggers that will cause him to react in a specific way to the assassination and his recovery.

This isn't changing his soul. This isn't making him a different person. It is merely nudging him toward a certain path, much as a con man on the street will strongly nudge his mark to pick a certain card. It is him. The him that could have been.

Who knows? Perhaps it is the him that would have been.

Gaotona would never have figured it out on his own, of course. His skill was faint in this area. Even if he'd been a master, he suspected he wouldn't have spotted Shai's work here. She explained in the book that her intention had been to be so subtle, so careful, that no one would be able to decipher her changes. One would have to know the emperor with extreme depth to even suspect what had happened.

With the notes, Gaotona could see it. Ashravan's near death would send him into a period of deep introspection. He would seek his journal, reading again and again the accounts of his youthful self. He would see what he had been, and would finally, truly seek to recover it.

Shai indicated the transformation would be slow. Over a period of years, Ashravan would become the man that he'd once seemed destined to be. Tiny inclinations buried deep within the interactions of his seals would nudge him toward excellence instead of indulgence. He would start thinking of his legacy, as opposed to the next feast. He would remember his people, not his dinner appointments. He would finally push the factions for the changes that he, and many before him, had noticed needed to be made.

In short, he would become a fighter. He would take that single—but so hard—step across the line from dreamer to doer. Gaotona could see it, in these pages.

He found himself weeping.

Not for the future or for the emperor. These were the tears of a man who saw before himself a *masterpiece*. True art was more than beauty; it was more than technique. It was not just imitation.

It was boldness, it was contrast, it was subtlety. In this book, Gaotona found a rare work to rival that of the greatest painters, sculptors, and poets of any era.

It was the greatest work of art he had ever witnessed.

Gaotona held that book reverently for most of the night. It was the creation of months of fevered, intense artistic transcendence—forced by external pressure, but released like a breath held until the brink of collapse. Raw, yet polished. Reckless, but calculated.

Awesome, yet unseen.

So it had to remain. If anyone discovered what Shai had done, the emperor would fall. Indeed, the very empire might shake. No one could know that Ashravan's decision to finally become a great leader had been set in motion by words etched into his soul by a blasphemer.

As morning broke, Gaotona slowly—excruciatingly—stood up beside his hearth. He clutched the book, that matchless work of art, and held it out.

Then he dropped it into the flames.

Postscript

IN WRITING CLASSES, I was frequently told, "Write what you know." It's an adage writers often hear, and it left me confused. Write what I know? How do I do that? I'm writing fantasy. I can't know what it's like to use magic—for that matter, I can't know what it's like to be female, but I want to write from a variety of viewpoints.

As I matured in skill, I began to see what this phrase meant. Though in this genre we write about the fantastic, the stories work best when there is solid grounding in our world. Magic works best for me when it aligns with scientific principles. Worldbuilding works best when it draws from sources in our world. Characters work best when they're grounded in solid human emotion and experience.

Being a writer, then, is as much about observation as it is imagination.

I try to let new experiences inspire me. I've been

lucky enough in this field that I am able to travel frequently. When I visit a new country, I try to let the culture, people, and experiences there shape themselves into a story.

Recently I visited Taiwan, and was fortunate enough to visit the National Palace Museum along with my editor Sherry Wang and translator Lucie Tuan to play tour guides. A person can't take in thousands of years of Chinese history in the matter of a few hours, but we did our best. Fortunately, I had some grounding in Asian history and lore already. (I lived for two years in Korea as an LDS missionary, and I then minored in Korean during my university days.)

Seeds of a story started to grow in my mind from this visit. What stood out most to me were the stamps. We sometimes call them "chops" in English, but I've always called them by their Korean name of *tojang*. In Mandarin, they're called *yìnjiàn*. These intricately carved stone stamps are used as signatures for many different Asian cultures.

During my visit to the museum, I noticed many of the familiar red stamps. Some were, of course, the stamps of the artists—but there were others. One piece of calligraphy was covered in them. Lucie and Sherry explained—ancient Chinese scholars and nobility, if they liked a work of art, would sometimes stamp it with their stamp too. One emperor in particular loved to do this, and would take beautiful sculptures or pieces of jade—centuries old—and have his stamp and perhaps some lines of his poetry carved into them.

What a fascinating mind-set. Imagine being a king, deciding that you particularly liked Michelangelo's *David*, and so having your signature carved across the chest. That's essentially what this was.

The concept was so striking, I began playing with a stamp magic in my head. Soulstamps, capable of rewriting the nature of an object's existence. I didn't want to stray too close to Soulcasting from the Stormlight world, and so instead I used the inspiration of the museum—of history—to devise a magic that allowed rewriting an object's past.

The story grew from that starting place. As the magic aligned a great deal with a system I'd been developing for Sel, the world where *Elantris* takes place, I set the story there. (I also had based several cultures there on our-world Asian cultures, so it fit wonderfully.)

You can't always write what you know—not exactly what you know. You can, however, write what you see.

Brandon Sanderson

Acknowledgments

A BOOK LIKE THIS goes out with one name on the cover, yet artwork is not created in a vacuum. What I create can only exist because of the numerous shoulders I rely upon.

I've mentioned elsewhere that this book came to be because of a trip I took to Taiwan. Many thanks go to Lucie Tuan and Sherry Wang, to whom the book is dedicated, for showing me around the city. Also, I'd like to thank Evanna Hsu and everyone else at Fantasy Foundation for making that trip such a powerful experience. Many thanks to Gray Tan (my Taiwan agent) who facilitated the trip, and to my U.S. agent Joshua Bilmes and everyone else at JABberwocky.

Jacob Weisman and Jill Roberts at Tachyon have been absolutely wonderful to work with, and I thank them for giving this work a home. Also, thank you to Marty Halpern for the copyedit and proofread. The great cover illustration comes from Alexander Nanitchkov, and I couldn't have asked for better.

Mary Robinette Kowal is responsible for the current structure of the novella; she helped me realize my original prologue wasn't the best for the integrity of the work. Moshe Feder went above and beyond his job description (at a different publisher) to offer me fantastic line edits, without which this book would have been much the poorer. I also got important feedback from Brian Hill, Isaac Stewart, and Karen Ahlstrom.

As always, I give loving thanks to my family, particularly my wife Emily. In addition, special thanks go out to the interpolated Peter Ahlstrom, who worked long hours on this project. (Even so far as to nudge me to get this acknowledgments page written after I'd forgotten to do so about a dozen times.)

You have my deepest gratitude, all of you.
Brandon

About the Author

BRANDON SANDERSON was born in 1975 in Lincoln, Nebraska. As a child Brandon enjoyed reading, but he lost interest in the types of titles often suggested to him, and by junior high he never cracked a book if he could help it. This changed when an eighth grade teacher gave him *Dragonsbane* by Barbara Hambly. Brandon thoroughly enjoyed this book, and went in search of anything similar. He discovered such authors as Robert Jordan, Melanie Rawn, David Eddings, Anne McCaffrey, and Orson Scott Card. Brandon continued to be an avid reader through junior high and high school. He liked epic fantasy so much that he even tried his hand at writing some. His first attempts, he says, were dreadful.

Brandon was working on his thirteenth novel when Moshe Feder at Tor Books bought the sixth he had written. Tor has published *Elantris*; the Mistborn trilogy and its follow-up, *The Alloy of Law*; *Warbreaker*; and *The Way of Kings*, the first in the planned ten-volume series The Stormlight Archive. He was chosen to complete Robert Jordan's Wheel of Time series: 2009's *The Gathering Storm* and 2010's *Towers of Midnight* will be followed by the final book in the series, *A Memory of Light*, in January 2013. Four books in his middle-grade *Alcatraz Versus the Evil Librarians* series were released by Scholastic, and his novella *Infinity Blade: Awakening* was an ebook bestseller for Epic Games accompanying their acclaimed *Infinity Blade* iOS video game series. Another novella, *Legion*, was released by Subterranean Press, and 2013 will bring two young adult novels, *The Rithmatist* from Tor and *Steelheart* from Delacorte.

The only author to make the short list for the David Gemmell Legend Award six times in four years, Brandon won that award in 2011 for *The Way of Kings* and was on the short list again in 2012 for *The Alloy of Law*. He has also won the Romantic Times Reviewers' Choice Award for Best Epic Fantasy twice and has been nominated three other years. He was twice nominated for the John W. Campbell Award for Best New Writer, and he won Audible.com's third annual Tournament of Audiobooks. He has hit the *New York Times* Hardcover Fiction Best-Seller List six times, with both Wheel of Time books hitting the #1 spot. *Towers of Midnight* was on the list for a Wheel of Time record eighteen straight weeks. *Alcatraz Versus the Evil Librarians* was optioned for film by DreamWorks Animation, *Mistborn* was optioned by Paloppa Pictures, *Legion* was optioned by Lionsgate, and *Steelheart* was optioned by FilmEngine. A Mistborn video game, *Mistborn: Birthright*, will be released by Little Orbit in 2013 for multiple platforms. Brandon's books have been published in over 20 languages, and he has won Spain's UPC Science Fiction Award.

Currently living in Utah with his wife and children, Brandon teaches creative writing at Brigham Young University. With Howard Tayler, Mary Robinette Kowal, and Dan Wells, he also hosts the twice Hugo-nominated writing advice podcast Writing Excuses, which has thrice won a Parsec Award.